THE HILLS ARE ALIVE

Something wasn't right. Fargo slowed to a walk. He didn't think they had seen him, but then again, all it would take was one warrior with eyes as sharp as a hawk's to look back at just the right moment.

His skin prickling, Fargo placed his hand on his Colt. He would go on a little ways yet, and if he didn't spot them, turn back.

The last Fargo saw of the six, they were winding between a pair of wooded hills. Both hills were about the same size and shape, and reminded him of a woman's breasts. He grinned at the notion, and thought of Rebecca Keever, of her full bosom and winsome figure.

The next moment Fargo promptly lost his grin when the trees to his right and the trees to his left disgorged shrieking warriors brandishing lances and notching arrows to sinew strings.

He had ridden right into a trap.

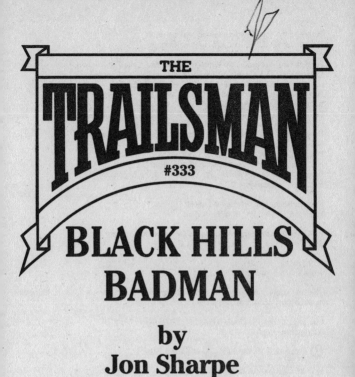

THE

TRAILSMAN

#333

BLACK HILLS
BADMAN

by
Jon Sharpe

Ⓢ
A SIGNET BOOK

SIGNET
Published by New American Library, a division of
Penguin Group (USA) Inc., 375 Hudson Street,
New York, New York 10014, USA
Penguin Group (Canada), 90 Eglinton Avenue East, Suite 700, Toronto,
Ontario M4P 2Y3, Canada (a division of Pearson Penguin Canada Inc.)
Penguin Books Ltd., 80 Strand, London WC2R 0RL, England
Penguin Ireland, 25 St. Stephen's Green, Dublin 2,
Ireland (a division of Penguin Books Ltd.)
Penguin Group (Australia), 250 Camberwell Road, Camberwell, Victoria 3124,
Australia (a division of Pearson Australia Group Pty. Ltd.)
Penguin Books India Pvt. Ltd., 11 Community Centre, Panchsheel Park,
New Delhi - 110 017, India
Penguin Group (NZ), 67 Apollo Drive, Rosedale, North Shore 0632,
New Zealand (a division of Pearson New Zealand Ltd.)
Penguin Books (South Africa) (Pty.) Ltd., 24 Sturdee Avenue,
Rosebank, Johannesburg 2196, South Africa

Penguin Books Ltd., Registered Offices:
80 Strand, London WC2R 0RL, England

First published by Signet, an imprint of New American Library,
a division of Penguin Group (USA) Inc.

First Printing, July 2009
10 9 8 7 6 5 4 3 2 1

The first chapter of this book previously appeared in *Beartooth Incident*, the three
hundred thirty-second volume in this series.

Copyright © Penguin Group (USA) Inc., 2009
All rights reserved

Ⓢ REGISTERED TRADEMARK—MARCA REGISTRADA

Printed in the United States of America

The Trailsman

Beginnings . . . they bend the tree and they mark the man. Skye Fargo was born when he was eighteen. Terror was his midwife, vengeance his first cry. Killing spawned Skye Fargo, ruthless, cold-blooded murder. Out of the acrid smoke of gunpowder still hanging in the air, he rose, cried out a promise never forgotten.

The Trailsman they began to call him all across the West: searcher, scout, hunter, the man who could see where others only looked, his skills for hire but not his soul, the man who lived each day to the fullest, yet trailed each tomorrow. Skye Fargo, the Trailsman, the seeker who could take the wildness of a land and the wanting of a woman and make them his own.

The Black Hills, 1861—woe to the white man who invaded the land of the Lakotas.

1

It was like looking for a pink needle in a green and brown haystack.

Or so Skye Fargo thought as he scanned the prairie for the girl. She would be easy to spot if it weren't for the fact there was so *much* prairie. A sea of grass stretched from Canada to Mexico, broken here and there by rivers and mountain ranges.

North of him, not yet in sight, were the Black Hills.

Fargo didn't like being there. He was in Sioux country, and the Sioux were not fond of whites these days. More often than not, any white they came across was treated to a quiver of arrows or had his throat slit and his hair lifted so it could hang from a coup stick in a warrior's lodge.

Fargo was white, but it was hard to tell by looking at him. His skin was bronzed dark by the relentless sun. He had lake-blue eyes, something no Sioux ever did. He wore buckskins. A white hat, a red bandanna, and boots were the rest of his attire. A Colt with well-worn grips was strapped around his waist. In an ankle sheath nestled an Arkansas toothpick. From his saddle scabbard jutted the stock of a Henry rifle.

Rising in the stirrups, Fargo squinted against the glare of the sun and raked the grass from east to west and back again. It wasn't flat, not this close to the Hills. A maze of gullies and washes made spotting her that much harder.

"Damn all kids, anyhow," Fargo grumbled out loud. He

gigged the Ovaro and rode on, vowing that there would be hell to pay when he got back to the party he was guiding.

A shrill whistle drew his gaze to a prairie dog. It had spotted him and was warning its friends.

Fargo swung wide of the prairie dog town. The last thing he needed was for the Ovaro to step into a hole and break a leg. He intended to keep the stallion a good long while. It was the best horse he ever rode. Often, it meant the difference between his breathing air or breathing dirt.

"Where could she have gotten to?"

Fargo had a habit of talking to himself. It came from being alone so much. He was a frontiersman, or as some would call him, a plainsman, although he spent as much time in the mountains as he did roaming the grasslands. Wide spaces, empty of people, was how he liked it.

He came to the crest of a knoll and drew rein again. Twisting from side to side, he still couldn't spot her. Frowning, he indulged in a few choice cuss words. He began to regret ever taking this job.

About to ride on, Fargo glanced down, and froze. Hoofprints showed he wasn't the first on that knoll. The tracks were made by unshod horses, which meant Indians, and in this instance undoubtedly meant Sioux. There had been five of them. They passed that way several days ago. That was good. They were long gone and posed no danger to the girl.

There were a lot of other dangers, though. Bears, wolves, cougars, rattlesnakes, all called the prairie home. Most times they left people alone, but not always, and it was the not always that worried him. To a griz she would be no more than a snack. A hungry wolf might decide to try something new. As for cougars, they'd kill and eat just about anything they could catch.

"The ornery brat," Fargo groused some more. He kept riding and was soon amid a maze of coulees.

Fargo could see the headlines now.

SENATOR'S DAUGHTER RIPPED APART
BY WILD BEAST!

Or

HUNTING TRIP ENDS IN TRAGEDY.

Or

FAMOUS TRAILSMAN LOSES CHILD
TO MEAT-EATER.

That last one was the likeliest. Journalists loved to write about him, often making up stories out of whole cloth. The more sensational the tale, the better. All to boost circulation. Were it up to him, he'd take every scribbler alive and throw them down a well.

Fargo rounded a bend, and drew rein. In the grass ahead lay something yellow and pink. Suspecting what it was, he dismounted and walked over, his spurs jingling. The girl's doll grinned up at him. He picked it up. The blond curls and pink dress were a copy of the girl and the dress she often wore.

She had been there and dropped the doll. That worried him. She never went anywhere without the thing. She even slept with it. She wouldn't run off and leave it.

A scream split the air.

Fargo was in the saddle before it died. He reined sharply in the direction the scream came from. Half a minute of hard riding and he found her at last. She wasn't alone.

Gertrude Keever had her back to a dirt bank and was kicking at the creatures trying to sink their teeth into her. There were two of them: coyotes. Ordinarily their kind stayed well shy of humans but this pair was scrawny. Either they were sickly or poor hunters, and they were hungry enough to go after Gerty.

Fargo drew his Colt and fired into the ground. He had nothing against the coyotes. They were only trying to fill their bellies. At the blast, one of them ran off. The other didn't even look up. It kept on snapping at the girl's legs and missed by a whisker.

"Kill this stupid thing, you simpleton!" the girl yelled.

Fargo almost wished the coyote had bit her. He fired from the hip and cored its head.

Gerty glared at him. "Took you long enough." She stepped to the dead coyote, squatted, and stuck a finger in the bullet hole. The she held her finger up and grinned as she watched the blood trickle down.

"What the hell are you doing?"

The girl held her finger higher for him to see. "Look. Isn't it pretty?"

Swinging down, Fargo walked over, gripped her elbow, and jerked her to her feet. "You damned nuisance. Wash your face with it, why don't you?"

"I'm going to tell Father on you. He won't like how you talk to me. He won't like it one bit."

Fargo sighed. For a thirteen-year-old, she was as big a pain as some women twice her age. "I'll do more than talk if you don't start showing some common sense."

"What do you mean?"

Fargo nodded at the dead coyote. "What the hell do you think I mean? You nearly got eaten. You can't go wandering off whenever you want. It's too damn dangerous."

"Oh, posh. You've been saying that since the first day and nothing has happened."

Fargo didn't point out that nothing happened because he made it a point to keep them safe. Instead, he shook her, hard. "You'll do as you're supposed to or I'll take you over my knee."

"You wouldn't!"

"Don't try me." Fargo hauled her to the Ovaro. He had

put up with her shenanigans because her father was paying him but there were limits to how much he'd abide.

Fargo had never met a girl like her. Gerty looked so sweet and innocent with her wide green eyes and golden curls, but she had a heart of pure evil. She was constantly killing things. Bugs, mostly, since they were about all she could catch. Although once, near the Platte, they came on a baby bird that had fallen from its nest, and Gerty beaned it with a rock. Her father thought it hilarious.

Not Fargo. He had seen her pull wings from butterflies and moths, seen her throw ants into the fire, seen her try to gouge out her pony's eyes when it didn't do what she wanted. He'd never met a child like her.

"What are you doing?"

"Taking you back."

Gerty stamped her foot. "I don't want to. I want to explore some more."

"Didn't that coyote teach you anything?" Fargo swung her onto the saddle and climbed on behind her. "Hold on to the horn."

"The what?"

"That thing sticking up in front of you." Fargo tapped his spurs and went up the side of the coulee, making a beeline for camp. The summer sun was warm on his face, the scent of grass strong.

Gerty swiveled her head to fix him with another glare. "I don't like you. I don't like you an awful lot."

"Good for you."

"My so-called mother does, though."

"She said that?" Fargo liked the senator's wife. She was quiet and polite, and she always spoke kindly to him. She also had the kind of body that made men drool.

"Forget about her. It's me who can't stand your guts."

"As if I give a damn." Fargo was alert for sign of the Sioux. Venturing into their territory was never the brightest of notions. But the senator had insisted on hunting in the notorious Black Hills.

"In fact, I'm starting to hate you."

"I'm sure I'll lose sleep over it."

Gerty was fit to burst her boiler. She flushed red with fury. "Don't you want to know why?"

"No."

"I'll tell you anyway. You're mean. You stopped me from poking my pony with that stick. You wouldn't let me kill that frog by the Platte River. And when I killed that baby bird you called me a jackass. Father didn't hear you but I did, as plain as day."

"You have good ears."

Gerty cocked her arm to punch him.

"I wouldn't," Fargo advised. "I hit a lot harder than you do."

"You wouldn't dare. Father would be mad. He won't pay you the rest of your money."

"Then I'll hit him."

Gerty laughed. "You don't know anything. Father is an important man. You hit him and he'll have you arrested."

Fargo motioned at the unending vista of prairie. "Do you see a tin star anywhere?" To his relief she shut up, but she simmered like a pot put on to boil. She was so used to getting her own way that when someone had the gall to stand up to her, she hated it.

Her father was to blame. Senator Fulton Keever was a big man in Washington, D.C. The senior senator from New York, Keever made a name for himself standing up for what the newspapers called "the little people." He was also reputed to be something of a hunter and had the distinction of bagging the biggest black bear ever shot in that state.

"What are those?" Gerty asked, pointing.

Fargo wanted to kick himself. He'd let his attention wander. He looked, and felt his pulse quicken. Four riders were silhouetted against the western horizon. They were too far off to note much detail but there could be no mistake; they were Sioux warriors. A hunting party, most likely, but they wouldn't hesitate to kill any whites they came across.

Fargo had to find cover before they spotted the Ovaro. A buffalo wallow was handy and he reined down into it.

"Land sakes." Gerty covered her mouth and nose and asked through her fingers, "What's that awful stink?"

"Buffalo piss."

"What?"

"Buffalo like to roll in the dirt. Sometimes they pee in it and get mud all over them to keep off the flies and whatnot."

"It smells terrible. Get me out of here this instant."

"We're not going anywhere just yet." Not until Fargo was good and sure the warriors were gone.

Twisting, Gerty poked him in the chest. "My father will hear of this. I'll tell him all about how you've treated me."

"That threat is getting old."

"You're a despicable person, do you know that?"

There had been times, admittedly few, when Fargo wondered what it would be like to have a wife and kids. He made a mental note that the next time he began to wonder, he'd think of Gerty. She was enough to make any man swear off kids for life.

"Why don't you say something? How can you stand the odor?"

"Quit flapping your gums and hold your breath and it won't be as bad." None of the buffalo tracks, Fargo saw, were fresh. Which was just as well. It wouldn't do to have a buff come along and take exception to their being there.

"Have I mentioned I'm starting to hate you?"

"Have I mentioned I don't give a damn?"

"I hope a rattlesnake bites you."

Fargo was commencing to regret ever agreeing to guide the Keevers. The senator was paying him almost twice what most guide jobs earned, but the money wasn't everything.

Fargo had been in Denver, gambling, when an older gentleman in a suit and bowler looked him up and asked if he would be so kind as to pay Senator Fulton Keever a visit at the Imperial. Fargo was on a losing streak anyway, so he went.

Keever had welcomed him warmly. It turned out the senator was on a hunting trip and needed a guide. Keever had heard Fargo was in town and sought him out. Fargo wasn't all that interested until Keever mentioned how much he was willing to pay.

"I have a question, you lump of clay," Gerty interrupted his musing.

"Hush, girl." Fargo was tired of her jabber.

"It's important."

"I doubt that."

"Are buffalo friendly?"

"About as friendly as you are."

"That buffalo over there doesn't look very friendly." Gerty pointed up at the rim.

Silhouetted against the sun was a bull buffalo.

2

"Oh, hell."

Fargo raised the reins but didn't use his spurs. Movement might provoke the bull into attacking. He waited for it to make up its mind what it was going to do. The wallow hadn't been used recently, and Fargo had seen no other sign of a herd's recent passage. So the bull might be by itself. No sooner did the thought cross his mind than two more bulls appeared behind the first.

It wasn't unusual. Bulls fought fiercely for their harems. Those that lost, or those not quite mature enough to do battle, often gathered in small herds of their own.

"There's more," Gerty said.

The total was now six. The first one stamped a hoof and shook its shaggy head, angry at the intrusion.

"Hold tight," Fargo cautioned, and took a gamble. He reined away from the bulls and rode at a walk toward the opposite rim. He hoped the buffalo would let them be, but the brutes were temperamental and hard to predict.

Gerty giggled. "They sure are funny-looking."

"Hush."

"I'm tired of you telling me that. You're not my father. I don't have to listen to you."

Fargo imagined the buffalo charging, and him throwing Gerty in its path, and he grinned. Not that he would. Sure, he'd done his share of what some folks would call wicked things in his life, but there was a line he wouldn't cross and killing children was one of them.

"Why does that one keep stomping its foot?"

"It doesn't like the sound of your voice."

"I don't believe you. You're just saying that so I'll shut up."

Which was true, but Fargo would be damned if he would admit it. They were near the top of the wallow. Once they reached the grass he would give the Ovaro its head.

Then two more buffalo appeared—in front of them.

Fargo drew rein. He hadn't counted on this. Like the others they were bulls. Hairy monsters, weighing upward of two thousand pounds when full grown, with a horn spread of three feet from tip to tip. They had few natural enemies. On rare occasions a wolf pack might bring down a crippled or old buff, and grizzlies were known to go after buffalo calves. But generally, buffalo were the lords of the prairie.

"They look almost as mean as you are."

"They're trying to decide whether to eat you," Fargo said as he reined to the right to swing wide of the pair ahead.

"Buffalo don't eat people, they eat grass. You're nothing but a big old liar."

"And you're a pain in the ass, so we're even." Her chatter was distracting him and Fargo couldn't afford to be distracted. He glanced at the other buffs across the wallow. They hadn't moved.

"Why don't you shoot one for our supper? You've shot others and I like the meat."

So did Fargo. He liked it even more than venison but not quite as much as he liked the delicious flesh of mountain lion.

"You're rude, do you know that? I asked you a question and you didn't answer."

Fargo resisted an urge to cuff her. They were almost out of the wallow. Another few moments and they could fly like the wind.

"Do you know what else you are? You're what Father calls a lout. Do you know what that is? A lout is a person with no manners. You have no manners." Gerty smiled sweetly.

"And you're a brat, so we're even."

Without warning, Gerty let out with a shrill, *"I hate you!"*

That was all it took; the two nearest buffalo charged.

Fargo used his spurs. The Ovaro exploded into motion and they were up and out of the wallow and flying across the flatland with the two huge buffalo in pursuit. Gerty clutched the saddle horn and squealed in fright. He gripped her arm to steady her and she bit his finger.

The buffalo were gaining. When they wanted to, the monsters could move incredibly fast.

Fargo used his spurs a second time. He held on to Gerty, intent on saving her despite herself.

For a while the issue was in doubt. The bulls stubbornly kept after them. Then the larger of the two came to a stop and the other followed suit, and the pair stood stomping and blowing and tossing their horns.

Fargo didn't slow. Not until he had gone several hundred yards more and he was sure it was safe.

"Let go of me," Gerty snapped. "I don't like people to touch me unless I say they can and I didn't say you could."

"Would you rather fall off?" Fargo remembered the warriors he had seen on the horizon. He gazed to the west but they were gone.

"You squeezed too hard. It hurts." Gerty rubbed her arm. "I'm going to ask Father to get rid of you. We don't need you, anyhow. That other man, Owen, knows just as much as you do, and he's a lot nicer to me."

Fargo frowned. Lem Owen was a fellow frontiersman, but there any resemblance ended. Owen was short and stubby and never, ever, bathed. On hot days he stank to high heaven.

Back East they had a saying that "cleanliness was next to godliness"; west of the Mississippi people were more fond of their sweat.

The real difference between Fargo and Owen was in their outlook. Fargo never killed unless he had to, even when it came to game. Owen loved to kill for killing's sake. A while back Owen made headlines by taking part in a wager with another hunter over who could shoot the most buffalo in a single day. The other man shot 204, Owen brought down 263. They left the buffs to rot.

There were other incidents. Once, drunk, Owen roped a dog and dragged it up and down a street for the fun of it. The dog died.

Another time, Owen heard about a farmer who had raised a buck from a fawn so that the buck was as tame as a kitten and would eat out of the farmer's hand. The buck also had antlers that were the talk of the territory. Owen decided he wanted the rack so he shot the buck dead one morning when the farmer called it in to eat, and when the farmer objected, Owen and a few of his friends beat the man senseless. The farmer was so scared, he didn't press charges.

Fargo was surprised Senator Keever had hired Owen. When he asked why, the senator shrugged and remarked that he needed men with experience, and there was no denying Owen knew the plains and mountains as well as any man alive, Fargo included.

"Didn't you hear me? I'm going to ask Father to get rid of you."

"Be my guest." Fargo spied the ribbon of trees that bordered the stream they had camped by. "I'd be happy to be shed of you."

"You would? Then I won't ask him. I don't want to do anything that will make you happy."

A tent had been pitched. The horses were in a string. A fire crackled, and the aroma of coffee filled the clearing. In addition to the senator and his wife and daughter, there were eleven men in the hunting party.

Rebecca Keever was pacing in front of the tent. The instant she saw Fargo and Gerty, she rushed to meet them, her dress clinging to her willowy legs. She had thick auburn hair and an oval face with high cheekbones and deep blue eyes. Her lips were small but full, and they parted now in a smile of relief. "You found her! Thank God."

Fargo reined up. Gripping Gerty's wrist, he swung her down before she had a chance to squawk or resist. "Here. Take her."

Rebecca held her daughter to her bosom. "Thank God. Don't ever wander off like that again. You had me worried sick."

"Don't you mean *us*, my dear?"

Senator Fulton Keever was an imposing figure. Six and a half feet tall in his bare feet, he favored expensive clothes and boots with high heels so that he seemed even taller. Although only in his forties, he had hair as white as snow. His face was broad and handsome. He carried himself with dignity, his shoulders always squared, his carriage erect. Now he came up and held out his arms and his wife handed Gerty to him. "How's my precious?"

Gerty beamed in delight, and hugged him. "I've had the most awful time."

"You're lucky Mr. Fargo was able to find you."

"It was him that made it awful. I didn't want to come back but he made me."

"He was doing his job."

"But he called me names and threatened to hit me." Gerty smacked her father on the shoulder. "Do something. Punish him. Have him whipped or something."

"I'm afraid it doesn't work that way," Senator Keever said. "I'd be voted out of office at the next election."

"You won't have him beaten for me?" Gerty let her resentment show. "I bet you're scared. He wears a gun and you don't so you won't do anything to make him mad."

"Gertrude!" Rebecca exclaimed.

"What else can it be?" Gerty said coldly. "Father always does what I ask. *Always*. Except get rid of that awful Fargo, and get rid of you."

Rebecca recoiled as if she had been slapped. "Gertrude Priscilla Keever, that will be enough. I'm your mother and you will treat me with the respect I deserve."

"There are mothers and there are mothers."

Fargo wondered what she meant by that. Were she his kid, he'd introduce her backside to his belt. Some people claimed that was crude and uncivilized, something "only a heathen Indian would do," as one man put it. Ironically, most Indians never hit their children. They believed it did lasting harm.

"Think you're funny, do you?" Rebecca was saying. "Well, I don't. For running off like that, you'll help the cook wash dishes the next three days. And you will be under your blankets by ten at night."

Gerty pressed against her father. "Wash dishes? Me? I've never washed a dish in my life."

"Fulton, tell her," Rebecca said.

"Ahh, now." Senator Keever pecked Gerty on the forehead and lowered her to the ground. "I don't think we have to go quite that far."

"What?"

"You heard me, my dear. She's young yet. Children her age like to explore. Yes, she strayed too far, and yes, Mr. Fargo had to go find her. But really, now. Must we punish the girl for acting her age? I say no. I say we should be thankful she's safe, and let it go."

The hurt in Rebecca's eyes said more than words ever could.

Senator Keever patted Gerty on the head. "There now.

All's well that ends well. Why don't you run along and play and we'll call you when supper is ready?"

Gerty pointed at Fargo. "What about him?"

"I've already said I'm not having him whipped. But I'll tell you what I'll do. When we return to civilization, I'll buy you whatever your little heart desires. A new dress, a new hat, a new pony since you're no longer fond of your old one. How does that sound?"

"I guess that's all right," Gerty said reluctantly.

They walked off and Fargo turned to tend to the Ovaro.

"Wait," Rebecca said, coming closer. "I want to thank you for what you did. How you found her so fast, I'll never know."

"I was lucky."

Rebecca had a lovely smile. "You're much too modest. My husband might not appreciate you but I do."

Fargo wondered how he should take that.

Gazing after Fulton and Gerty, Rebecca sighed. "I try to rear her right. I truly do. But you saw how he is. He spoils her. He spoils her terribly. Anything she wants, all she has to do is say so. It's been like that since she learned to talk."

Fargo was puzzled by why she was telling him this. "Your family squabbles are none of my concern, ma'am."

"True. But in this instance it's more than a squabble. You've made an enemy, Mr. Fargo."

"You'll pardon me if I don't tremble in my boots."

"Don't take her lightly, I warn you. She's a shark, that one. And she never forgets or forgives a slight."

"She's thirteen years old."

"So? Just because she's a child doesn't mean she won't figure out a way to get back at you." Rebecca leaned so close she was practically breathing on his neck. "Let me tell you a story. Back home we had a gardener, a most wonderful man. Kindly. Thoughtful. You couldn't ask for better. One day he caught Gerty cutting some of my roses. She had found his shears."

Fargo had little interest in her tale but he patiently waited for her to finish while roving his gaze from her neck to her toes, admiring her full bosom and the sweep of her thighs.

"He took them from her and scolded her, and do you know what she did? She kicked him in the shins. Without thinking, he slapped her." Rebecca was whispering now. "Gerty ran to Fulton and had the poor man fired."

"She's a firebrand," Fargo said dryly.

"There's more. The gardener was devastated. He'd worked for us for years. He begged to keep his job. He pleaded. Fulton might have given in if not for Gerty."

"And?" Fargo prompted when she didn't go on.

"The gardener went to collect his things. Everyone thought he left the estate. But the next morning a maid found him out by the roses with the pruning shears sticking out of his chest."

Fargo looked at her. "How did it happen?"

"It was ruled an accident. That he tripped and fell on the shears as he was about to hang them on a nail. But between you and me, that just won't wash. He was always careful with his tools."

"Are you saying Gerty did it?"

Rebecca shrugged. "Someone did. No one else had a motive. So watch your back from here on out. Watch it very closely."

3

The black bear lumbered along in search of food. It was following its nose, as bears always did. It had no idea it was
being watched.

The broken country was ideal for game. Bear and deer
were plentiful. So were antelope but they were hard to spot
and a lot harder to shoot. The wariest critters on God's green
earth, was how an old-timer once described them. Fargo
agreed.

"What do you think? Do you want to take a shot or
not?"

Senator Fulton Keever was studying the bear through a
spyglass. "It's a big one, Mr. Owen. I'll grant you that. But
I'm after trophies. I want a head I can hang on my wall and
boast about to my colleagues."

Fargo frowned. He'd spent the better part of an hour
tracking that bear. Most hunters would rate it more than big
enough.

"I suppose I could use it for practice." Senator Keever
held the spyglass out to Lem Owen and Owen took it and
handed Keever his hunting rifle.

Fargo saw no need for Owen to be there but the senator
wanted him along. One of Owen's pards came too, a weasel
called Lichen. Skinny and sallow, Lichen wore a broad-
bladed knife high in a brown leather sheath, and carried a
Sharps. He had the habit of chewing on blades of grass.

The senator had nearly a dozen rifles. No hunter needed

that many but Keever was putting money in Fargo's poke so Fargo didn't say anything. The rifle Keever was holding at the moment was a British model made by a well-known Brit gunsmith named Joseph Whitworth. Around the campfire one evening, the senator had mentioned that Whitworth's guns were highly sought after. "They cost more than most people earn in a year." Keever had stroked the rifle, which he was cleaning at the time. "He custom-made this to my specifications. With it I can shoot a bee out of the air at a hundred yards."

Fargo doubted that. But he was impressed by the thin tube attached to the top of the barrel. It was a spyglass in itself, enabling the shooter to see an animal as clearly as if he were standing next to it.

Now, Keever raised the rifle to his shoulder.

"Hold on."

Keever glanced up. "Is something the matter, Mr. Fargo?"

"That bear has as much right to go on breathing as you or me. If all you want is practice, shoot a tree."

"Are you serious?"

"If you did shoot it, then what?" Fargo asked.

The senator's brow puckered. "I'm not quite sure I understand. I'll shoot it and it will be dead. What more is there?"

"You'll just leave it there for the buzzards and the coyotes?"

Keever acted considerably surprised. "I must say, I never expected this from you, of all people. You have a reputation for being not only a fine tracker but a superb hunter in your own right. How can you be so squeamish over killing a bear?"

"The game I shoot, I use. I eat the meat. Sometimes I cure the hides and sell or trade them."

"That's what is bothering you? An issue easily solved. We'll butcher the bear and pack the meat to camp. Would that make you happy?"

Lem Owen snorted. "That's an awful lot of bother to go to, if you ask me. If I were in charge, Senator, I'd let you kill whatever you want, whenever you want."

"That'd decent of you. But Mr. Fargo is, and it would please me greatly if you would remember that."

"Your choice. I just hope it doesn't turn out to be the wrong one."

Fargo turned. This wasn't the first time Owen had implied he could do a better job as guide. "I don't get many complaints."

"You're making a fuss over a lousy bear."

"Too bad there's not a couple of hundred so you can shoot them like you did all those buffalo."

Owen chuckled. "There must be a million of the damn things. I could have dropped them all day and all night and it wouldn't make a difference."

"It would to the Indians who rely on the herds to live."

Owen's eyes widened. "Listen to yourself. Who in hell cares what redskins think? You know, I'd heard you were an Injun lover. But I never figured you for stupid."

Fargo hit him, a solid right cross to the jaw that knocked Owen against Lichen. Both men stumbled, and Owen would have fallen if Lichen hadn't caught him and held him up.

"What on earth!" Senator Keever exclaimed.

Owen shook himself and put a hand to his chin. Then, swearing, he clawed for the Remington revolver on his hip.

In the blink of an eye Fargo's Colt was up and out. They all heard the click of the hammer being thumbed back.

Owen turned to stone. His throat bobbed, and he said, "Hold on, now, hoss. There's no call to blow out my wick."

"Take your hand off your revolver."

Forcing a crooked grin, Owen obeyed. "I wouldn't really have drawn on you. I was mad, is all, you slugging me like that."

"When you go around insulting people that's what hap-

19

pens." Fargo let down the hammer and twirled the Colt into his holster.

Senator Keever stood. "Enough of this. I hired the two of you and I expect you to get along. Mr. Fargo, I've noticed that you're not overly fond of Mr. Owen. Mr. Owen, I'm aware that you don't think highly of Mr. Fargo. Whatever the cause of this silliness, either behave like adults or leave my employ."

"I'm all for getting along with folks," Owen said.

Fargo almost laughed in his face. Owen was the kind to smile while stabbing a person in the back. If ever there was such a thing as a human sidewinder, Lem Owen filled the bill.

"Mr. Fargo?" the senator prompted.

"What?"

"Your turn. Do you agree to get along with Mr. Owen for the duration of our hunt?"

"So long as he doesn't insult me, we'll get along fine."

"That's not what I asked," Keever said curtly. "I want your word that you will be on your best behavior."

"I'll do as I damn well please." Fargo took a step and poked Owen in the chest. "And so long as I'm guiding this outfit, I don't want any more guff out of you."

"Or what? You'd cut me loose in Sioux country? That's not very white of you."

Fargo almost hit him a second time.

"If word got out that you abandoned a white man in the Black Hills, there's not a soul alive who would hire you."

Senator Keever was staring in the direction of the black bear. "Look at what your bickering has done. You've made me lose my shot. The bear has gone into cover. We'll have to follow it in."

Up ahead, an isolated bluff was fringed by woodland. The undergrowth was particularly thick. Somewhere in there was their quarry.

They climbed on their mounts and rode to within fifty yards of the woods. Fargo dismounted, saying, "I'll come with you, Senator. Owen and Lichen will watch the horses." The Sioux were as fond of stealing horses as they were of counting coup.

"It'll take forever to flush that bear with just the two of you," Owen objected.

"An excellent point," Senator Keever agreed. "You may tag along. But remember what I said about behaving."

Fargo shucked his Henry from the saddle scabbard and levered a round into the chamber.

Owen had a .58 caliber rifle made by Parker, Snow and Company. They were supposedly accurate as could be but were single-shot.

The senator was wiping dust from his Whitworth. "Shall we bait the beast, gentlemen?" He grinned and made for the trees.

"We should stick together," Fargo proposed. For two reasons. First, he wanted Owen where he could see him; rumor had it that Owen wasn't above shooting people he disliked in the back. Second, he had yet to take the senator's measure as a hunter. Keever might have nerves of iron—or he might be prone to panic if the bear charged.

"Whatever for?" was the senator's reply. "We're all of us armed, and good shots. We can cover more ground by separating." As he spoke he bore to the right. "Good luck."

Owen bore to the left.

Leaving Fargo to stop and stare after them in mild frustration. Since arguing was pointless, he shrugged and made for the bluff.

That was the thing with guide work. Sometimes those he guided had enough sense to listen. Others were jackasses and did as they pleased, and often as not paid a high price for their folly.

The woods were alive with wildlife. A robin warbled high

in an oak. Sparrows flitted gaily. A ribbon snake crawled off at his approach, and shortly thereafter a wasp buzzed his ear. Tracks showed there were deer to be had. Larger prints were courtesy of elk.

Above the forest canopy reared the bluff. Long ago part of the near side had broken away, creating a slope littered with boulders. It went almost to the top. From up there a man would have a good view of the entire woods.

Fargo had lost sight of the senator and Owen. The skin between his shoulder blades prickling, he moved silently, alert for sign of them, especially Lem Owen. A twig crunched off to his left.

Instantly, Fargo crouched and tucked the Henry to his shoulder. It could be anything but he wasn't taking chances. He waited with the patience of an Apache for what or who to show it—or him—self, but nothing appeared. Warily, he stalked on.

Fargo wasn't too worried about the bear. Black bears usually avoided people. Likely as not, it would run when it saw them. But there was that one time in ten when black bears proved they could be as ferocious as grizzlies.

Close up, the bluff was gigantic. Fargo stepped from the trees and craned his neck. It was a two-hundred-foot climb, at least. He started up, glancing over his shoulder every few yards, just in case. At one point he thought he glimpsed someone off among the trees to the right; that would be the senator.

Gusts of wind stirred the whangs on Fargo's buckskins. He came to a flat boulder about waist high and climbed up for a look-see. He was higher than the tops of the trees and could see Lichen and the horses. But of Keever and Owen, there was no sign.

Hopping down, Fargo resumed climbing. The higher he went, the steeper it became. Loose dirt dribbled from under his boots. Dislodged stones rattled. He skirted several boulders and was within a pebble's toss of the top when a crow took wing from the woods below, cawing loudly. He looked, but whatever startled it into flight was well hidden.

The slope ended five feet below the rim. Raising both arms, Fargo slid the Henry over, then jumped, hooked his elbows, and with a lithe swing, gained the summit. He picked up the Henry as he rose. The top of the bluff was as flat as a flapjack and dotted with slabs of rock the size of covered wagons.

The view was spectacular. Prairie surrounded the hub of woodland for as far as the eye could see to the east, west, and south. To the north were the Black Hills.

Fargo walked along the rim, scouring the vegetation below. He saw Keever moving through dense growth. He didn't spot Owen. He was bending for a better look when something buzzed his ear. This time it wasn't a wasp. It was an arrow, and it came from *behind* him.

Diving flat, Fargo twisted and brought the Henry up. A shadow dappled one of the slabs, moving away from him.

Heaving upright, Fargo gave cautious chase. The warrior who loosed the shaft might have friends.

Rock slabs were all around. In the dust was the clear imprint of a foot clad in a moccasin.

Fargo wondered how the warrior got up there. He hadn't seen tracks on the slope. His back to a slab, he sidled to the other side. Then it was on to the next. It was slow going. Eventually, near the opposite rim, the boulders ended. Crouching, he peered over.

This side wasn't as steep. A well-defined game trail wound to the bottom. Almost to the end of it was a lone warrior on horseback. The style of his hair and his buckskins warned Fargo the man was a member of the one tribe he wanted to avoid: the Sioux. The warrior glanced up and smiled in grim defiance. Then he used a quirt on his mount.

"Damn."

Fargo jerked the Henry to his shoulder. He had time for one clear shot. He fixed a bead on the center of the warrior's back—and couldn't squeeze the trigger. Fargo never liked to back shoot. Yes, the warrior tried to kill him, but he was white, and an invader.

Lowering the Henry, Fargo stood there until the warrior and his mount were specks on the horizon. Then he retraced his steps.

Keever had disappeared again.

Owen might as well be invisible.

Fargo thought he had spotted one or the other in the middle of the woods. But it was something else, a black mass that detached itself from a patch of shadow Its shape left no doubt. The black bear had been lying up in a thicket but now it was on the move. Its head was low to the ground as if it were sniffing—or *stalking*.

Fargo leaned farther out.

Senator Keever was twenty yards from the bruin, blissfully unaware of his danger. The bear, though, now had its eyes locked on him.

Cupping a hand to his mouth to shout a warning, Fargo took one more step. The next moment the ground gave out under him and he plummeted over the edge.

4

An outcropping swept toward him. Instinctively, Fargo grabbed at it and was brought up short. The jolt nearly tore his arm from the socket. He couldn't use his other hand, though; he was holding the Henry and refused to let it go, no matter what.

His body dangling, Fargo looked down. He had to be a hundred and eighty feet above the ground, if not more. It was a straight drop to boulders at the bottom. He wouldn't survive the fall.

Fargo tried to brace his feet against the cliff. He jabbed with his toes, seeking a crack or a hole that would bear his weight, but try as he might he couldn't gain purchase. His boots kept slipping. Each time they did, he nearly lost his grip.

As it was, Fargo's shoulder was screaming for relief and his arm was in agony. He couldn't hold on much longer.

The seconds crawled into a minute. His fingers began to weaken. Gritting his teeth, he clamped on harder. He refused to give up. Death might claim him but not without a struggle.

It was then that a strange thing happened. A pair of buckskin pants came sailing over the edge and smacked the cliff next to him. He blinked in surprise, and saw that the pants were tied to a buckskin shirt. From above came a voice, the last voice in the world he expected to hear.

"Hook your rifle to the belt!"

A belt was secured to the end of the pant leg, and a loop

had been rigged for the Henry. But could Fargo do it one-handed? He tried three times before he succeeded in sliding the barrel through the loop as far as the breech. It wasn't snug but it would have to do.

"Let go and I'll pull it up!"

Fargo glanced up. The face peering down at him showed concern, which in itself was remarkable. He nodded and released the Henry, then gripped the outcropping with both hands.

The pants rose, taking the rifle with them. For a few anxious moments he feared it would slip out and drop and be shattered, but no, his rescuer got it up and over.

"Your turn! Watch the knot!"

Down came the pants/shirt/belt "rope." The knot, where the pants were tied to the shirt, bulged like a fist. Would it hold? Fargo took the gamble. He grabbed the pants with one hand and then the other. The knot started to slip. He could see it shrinking. He tensed, thinking it would come undone, but just when it seemed his luck had run out, the knot caught.

"Hang on! Try not to move too much!"

Fargo rose, but oh-so-slowly. It had to be hard on the man pulling him. And the man had to be strong. Stronger than he thought.

Inch by snail-paced inch, Fargo was hiked higher until he was close enough to the rim to touch it. A brawny hand was lowered and iron fingers gripped his wrist.

"Get ready."

Fargo was yanked upward. He flung his arms nd over, wedged his elbows on the rim, and swung onto his knees.

"Finally." Lem Owen was in the dirtiest pair of long underwear any human ever wore. He lay on his back, puffing from his exertion, his bare feet bleeding where he had pressed them against the rocks.

"I'm obliged."

Owen waved a hand as if to say it was nothing.

"I mean it," Fargo said. Here he thought the man hated him, and Owen went and saved his life.

Owen grinned between gasps. "I never got undressed so fast in my life. But I couldn't think of what else to do. I didn't have a rope."

"I'm in your debt."

"Us white men have to stick together," Owen joked, then said, "Besides, the senator wouldn't like it if you were to get yourself killed."

Fargo pushed to his feet and turned to peer over the cliff. This time he was careful not to step too close to the edge.

"What is it?" Owen asked, sitting up.

"The last I saw, the black bear was stalking him." Fargo saw no sign of the politician or the beast. He unhooked his Henry from Owen's belt, tossed Owen his clothes, and bolted for the slope. He barely reached it when a tremendous roar rose from below, followed by the crack of a shot.

Fargo descended as fast as was safe. It was so steep, a single misstep would send him tumbling. He was breathing hard when he came to the bottom and flew in among the trees. "Keever! Where are you?"

There was no answer.

Fargo began moving in ever wider circles, seeking some sign. He kept calling out the senator's name. Then he rounded a pine and came on a small clearing and two still forms. "Damn."

The black bear was sprawled on its belly. Its head was bent to one side, ringed by a scarlet pool, and its long tongue lay limp over its lower teeth. From under the bear poked a pair of legs—human legs.

Fargo warily circled around. Keever's head and part of a shoulder jutted from under the other side of the bear. The senator's eyes were closed and he didn't appear to be breathing.

"Son of a bitch." Fargo poked the black bear with the

Henry. It appeared to be dead. Kneeling, he clasped Keever's wrist to feel for a pulse.

Senator Keever's eyes snapped open. "About time someone got here. Where have you been?"

"I had problems of my own." Fargo bent to try to see the senator's chest. He envisioned clawed and torn flesh, the ribs exposed, and worse.

"I can hardly breathe but otherwise I feel fine." Keever struggled to move. "Get this brute off me, will you?"

The bear had to weigh upward of five hundred pounds. Fargo drew his Colt and placed it in the senator's hand.

"What's this for?"

"Until I get back. I don't see your rifle anywhere." Fargo rose and dashed across the clearing.

"Wait! Don't leave me like this! Where are you going?"

"To get help." Fargo ran faster. He didn't like leaving the senator alone but he couldn't lift the bear by himself. He doubted he could get it off even if Owen helped. So he ran, and when at last he broke from the trees, Lichen and the horses were where they should be. He wasted no time in explanations but swung onto the Ovaro and told Lichen to bring the others. A rake of his spurs, and he galloped back into the woods.

Keever had company. Owen was hunkered next to him and they were talking heatedly about something but stopped when Fargo burst into the clearing. He drew rein so hard that the stallion slid to a stop. Vaulting down, he had his rope in hand when he reached the bear.

"So that's where you went," Keever said.

Owen was dressed again. He gave the bear a smack, and grinned. "Can you believe this? Pinned under a bear! He'll be the laughingstock of all his high and mighty friends if they hear of it."

"Which they never will," Keever said harshly. "I'm relying on your discretion, the both of you."

Owen snorted. "Hell, I don't even know what that is. But if you want me to keep my mouth shut, I will. For an extra hundred dollars."

"Is that all you ever think of? Money?"

"I think of women a lot. But the kind of women I like takes money to get to know. That hundred dollars won't buy me but two nights of heaven. I can always use more."

Fargo was walking around the black bear. It was obvious the senator wasn't gravely hurt. But if they weren't careful about how they got the bear off, he might be. Fargo stepped to where one of the bear's rear legs protruded and began tying the rope as tight as he could.

Lem Owen came around. "I savvy what you're up to. Two horses would be better. I'll fetch mine."

Just then Lichen arrived with the rest. Owen climbed on his animal, uncoiled his rope, and tossed an end to Fargo. Fargo tied it to the bear's other rear leg, then swung onto the Ovaro and lifted the reins.

"Nice and easy does it."

Senator Keever called out, "What are you two up to? I can't see from here. The bear's backside is in the way."

"Hold real still," Fargo cautioned. "We're about to drag the bear off you."

Owen laughed. "Say, Senator? When we start pulling, watch out that the bear doesn't snag a tooth or claw. You could lose skin, or maybe what you used to bring your little Gerty into the world."

Fargo was surprised Keever didn't take exception. Turning the Ovaro broadside to the bear, he dallied the rope around the saddle and glanced at Owen, who had done the same with his. "Ready? On the count of three."

The Ovaro and the dun strained and the ropes grew taut. Bit by bit the bear slid backward. Its open mouth and head left blood and fluid on the senator's shirt and jacket.

Keever was a statue. His rifle, it turned out, was next to

him. He didn't move until the bear's head slid over his ankles. Then he rose on his elbows and looked down at himself. "I appear to be no worse for wear. But my clothes are a terrible mess."

"You were damned lucky," Owen said. "A black bear ain't a griz but it can rip a man apart without half trying."

Fargo climbed down. He offered his hand and helped the senator to stand. There were no bite marks, no cuts, not so much as a tear in the senator's clothes. He nodded at the dead bruin. "Mind telling us what happened?"

"Not at all." Keever commenced brushing himself off. "It tried to sneak up on me but I heard it. When it charged, I shot it in the head. But the beast was so close, it rammed into me before I could get out of the way and fell on top of me."

Fargo reconstructed the event in his mind. "So the bear was almost on top of you when you heard it?"

"Actually, it was in the trees there." Keever pointed at the woods. "I heard it when it stepped on a downed tree limb and the limb broke."

Fargo calculated the distance. "That's a good thirty feet."

"More like forty." Keever smoothed his bloodstained jacket and ran a hand through his hair. "How do I look?"

"Wait a minute." Fargo needed to hear more. Something wasn't adding up. "The bear was forty feet off when it charged? And you only got off one shot? How close was it when you fired?"

"Oh, I'd say five or six feet."

"What the hell?" Owen said.

Fargo didn't understand it, either. "Why did you wait so long to shoot? You could have put two or three shots into it in that time." Even with a single-shot rifle.

Senator Keever gave them his best politician's smile. "That wouldn't be very sporting, now would it?"

Both Fargo and Owen said at the same time, "Sporting?"

"Gentlemen, gentlemen." Keever chortled at their confusion. "What do you take me for? I'm not one of those hunters who likes to sit a thousand yards off and drop a buffalo. Or wait up in a tree for a buck to come by. No, I like my contests to be fair."

"Contests?" Owen repeated.

"Yes. A battle of skill versus brawn, of courage versus savagery. To put it more simply, I like the animal to have as much a chance to kill me as I do to kill it. Most of the time, anyway."

"That's plumb stupid," Owen said.

"Think what you will. I pride myself on always giving the other fellow, or the other animal, an even break. Where was the challenge in shooting the bear when it was forty feet away? I let it get close enough to use its teeth and claws, and then I shot it."

"You do this a lot?" Fargo wanted to know.

"Almost always. It's how I test myself, how I take my own measure as a man. Surely the two of you can understand?"

"Stupid, stupid, stupid," Owen said.

"I don't do it all the time. Now and then I'll want a special trophy so much, I'll settle for killing the animal any way I can."

"Don't take this personal, Senator," Owen said, "but you're running around with an empty wagon between your ears."

"And you?" Senator Keever appealed to Fargo. "Do you think it ridiculous of me, too?"

Fargo was about to say yes but Keever didn't give him the chance.

"Consider, gentlemen, the lives you live. Day in, day out, you roam the raw frontier. You never know from one day to the next what you'll run into. Hostiles, wild beasts, the elements, all sorts of things can kill you. Yet you meet each day as the challenge it is without flinching."

Owen glanced at Fargo. "What the hell is he talking about?"

"Courage, Mr. Owen. The very core of what makes a man a man. With it, we can surmount any obstacle. Without it, we are mice in human guise."

"There must be a better way to test yourself," Fargo said.

"Such as? In combat, perhaps? The United States isn't at war right now or I would seek an officer's commission. How else, then? By gambling? Cards have never appealed to me. The outcome is more chance than anything. What does that leave? Some sport, perhaps? Golf or rowing or maybe baseball? Hitting a little ball with a stick strikes me as about the most unmanly activity on the planet."

"You sure have a way with words," Owen praised him.

Fargo folded his arms across his chest. "Why didn't you tell me all this before you hired me?"

"Because you might have refused to guide me and I wanted you and only you."

"Why?"

Instead of answering, Senator Keever stepped to the bear and patted its shoulder. "A fine adversary, if I say so myself. Next I want to shoot a bull buffalo and after that a grizzly."

"Are you going to pull the same stunt with them?" Owen asked.

"Of course."

"It was nice knowing you."

"I'll do my best not to get myself killed." As an afterthought the senator added, "Or either of you killed, as well."

5

Gerty threw down her fork and stamped her foot. "I hate deer meat! I hate it, hate it, hate it! I hate rabbit meat, too. Deer or rabbit. Rabbit or deer. Over and over and over."

"You can always go hungry," Fargo said to make her madder. He had been invited to supper with the Keevers. The senator had brought a folding table along and insisted his family use it for each and every meal.

Rebecca was swallowing tea, and coughed.

"Did you hear him, Father?" Gerty asked. "Did you hear how he talks to me? Yet you won't get rid of him like I've asked you."

"Now, now, child," Fulton Keever tried to soothe her. "I've explained before that Mr. Fargo is indispensable. Which means I can't do without him."

"I know what it means," Gerty declared. "I might be young but I'm not stupid."

Fargo couldn't let it go. "That's one opinion." All during the meal she had criticized him, carping that he didn't chew with his mouth closed, that he drank water like a horse, that he didn't use the right spoon when he had soup. It got so, Fargo would dearly love to chuck her off a cliff and see if she bounced.

"He's doing it again, Father."

Senator Keever sighed. "Mr. Fargo, must you? You're a grown man. It's beneath you to bait her."

Rebecca came to Fargo's defense. "She's been picking on him all evening. Surely you noticed?"

"A child's antics, nothing more," Keever said indulgently. "And I should think you would have more sympathy for a member of your own family."

"Gertrude means the world to me. You know that. But it wouldn't hurt if she learned some manners."

Gerty's mouth twisted in a cruel smirk. "You wouldn't say that if you were my real mother."

At last Senator Keever showed a flash of anger. "Enough, child. I made you promise never to bring that up, remember?"

"Real mother?" Fargo's curiosity had been piqued. He was under the impression Rebecca was the only wife Keever ever had. Which meant the senator had been tempted by a greener pasture.

Keever raised his napkin from his lap and slapped it down on the table. "Now see what you've done, Gertrude? There are some lapses I won't tolerate, and this is one of them." He looked around as if to make sure no one else could hear him. "I want your solemn word, Mr. Fargo, that you won't repeat what I'm about to tell you. Not to another living soul ever."

"You have it," Fargo said.

"I was very close to another woman once. Her name was Priscilla. We weren't married but we took it for granted that we would one day tie the knot."

Fargo saw a change in Rebecca's expression. One thing was obvious; she didn't like this talk of the "other woman."

The senator gazed off into the dark. "Priscilla would be seated at this table now but for the unforeseen. You see, she became in the family way. I was all for marrying her but God had other ideas." Keever's eyes mirrored sorrow. "She came down with consumption."

Fargo felt genuine sympathy. Consumption claimed a lot of folks. Some said it was the leading killer in New England

and other parts of the country, more so than any other disease.

"The doctors tried their best but there was nothing they could do." Keever stopped and turned to Gerty. "Why don't you go play? Maybe take your doll over by the fire for a while."

"I don't want to."

"I wasn't asking, I was telling you. It's time for grown-up talk and you're not an adult yet."

"If it's about my real mother I have the right to hear."

Keever grew stern. "I'm a lawyer, not you. I know what your rights are. Now go get your doll and sit by the fire. Or so help me I'll take the doll from you and not give it back until we're home."

Sulking, Gerty climbed down and went into their tent. She came back out holding her doll and muttering under her breath. Giving her father a withering glance, she went over to the fire.

"My darling girl," Senator Keever said. "She acts too big for her britches sometimes." He scratched his chin. "Now where was I? Oh, yes. I was telling you about Priscilla. She hung on as long as she could. Every day the doctors bled her and sweated her but it didn't help. Finally, about a month before the baby was due, she succumbed. But right before she died, the doctors cut Gerty out of her." Keever brushed at his face as if to dispel the memory. "So there I was. I had a child but no wife. But as fate would have it, I met Rebecca the very next week. One thing led to another, and when Gerty was four months old, Rebecca agreed to marry me."

Rebecca smiled, a thin smile that didn't touch her eyes.

"Now you know what my daughter meant," Keever said to Fargo. "I trust you will stand by your word and not reveal my secret to a living soul. It could ruin me politically."

Fargo didn't see how and said so.

"That shows how naïve you are. A politician must be above reproach, sir. My constituents expect me to be a model of moral and ethical behavior. In short, I must be perfect in all my ways or they will vote me out of office."

"You're human like the rest of us."

Senator Keever smiled. "You know that and I know that but try telling it to the Ladies Quilting Society or a church group. Were they to learn I had a child out of wedlock it would be the scandal of the century."

Fargo hadn't considered that aspect. Politicians had it harder than he reckoned.

"Now, if you will excuse me." Keever pushed back his chair. "I'll go keep my wonderful child company for a while."

Fargo gulped the last of the coffee in his cup. To make small talk, he said to Rebecca, "You have a fine family, ma'am."

"Oh, please. My so-called husband is a pompous ass and my so-called daughter is the biggest brat alive and will no doubt grow up to be the biggest bitch alive, as well."

Fargo didn't know what to say so he said nothing.

"I see I've shocked you. I'd apologize for my strong language but I meant every word." Rebecca leaned over and lowered her voice. "Take Fulton's account with a large grain of salt."

"Care to explain?"

"No. I've said too much as it is." Rebecca rose. "Be careful, Mr. Fargo. Be very careful. Things aren't as they seem. You've been nice to me so I'm giving you fair warning."

"I could use more details," Fargo said.

"You should leave. Now. Get on your horse and ride off and don't look back. Otherwise, you could very well wind up dead." Rebecca glanced apprehensively toward the others, then wheeled and strode into the tent. "I bid you good night," she said as the flap closed behind her.

Fargo was dumbfounded. She sounded sincere. He wondered what she meant by that "dead" business? He refilled his cup, and pondered. It could be she was worried about the Sioux. He didn't blame her. He was worried about the Sioux, too, especially after nearly taking an arrow in the back. That reminded him. Rising, he went over to the other fire.

Owen and Lichen and half a dozen others were hunkered around it. They stopped talking as he came up.

"I want an extra man to keep watch tonight and every night from here on out."

"You do, huh?" Owen snickered.

Lichen said, "One has been enough so far. Why should we have to lose more sleep?"

"I saw a Sioux warrior today not far from here."

That got them. Every last one sat up as if prodded with a pitchfork. Owen asked, "Why didn't you say anything sooner?"

"We're in Sioux country. You should have expected it." Especially, Fargo reflected, the closer they got to the Black Hills.

"I don't like those red heathens," a rawhide-complexioned gent by the name of Wiley mentioned. "There's nothing they like more than lifting white hair unless maybe it's slitting a white throat."

"You'll post the extra men?" Fargo said to Owen.

"Sure. And maybe you should make clear what we're to do if they pay us a visit? Do we shoot them on sight or would you rather we don't give in to itchy trigger fingers without your say-so?"

"Only shoot to kill if you have to." Fargo turned to go.

"Say," Owens said quietly. "About that disagreement you and me had earlier. No hard feelings? I might have been a little rude."

Fargo considered pinching himself to make sure he was awake. "It's over and done with."

"Good. I admire an hombre who doesn't hold a grudge." Owen held out his calloused hand. "How about we shake?"

Fargo could hold a grudge as good as the next man, but he shook, anyway. Again he went to leave.

"Hold on there, mister," Lichen said. "Folks say you've lived with the Sioux. Is that true?"

Fargo nodded.

"Then you must know them pretty well. Why don't you pay one of their villages a visit and ask them to leave us be?"

Owen said, "The senator wouldn't want him to do that."

"Why not? Injuns are always willing to bend backward for Injun lovers like Fargo, here."

Fargo kicked him, a short, hard kick to the chest that knocked Lichen flat on his back. Instantly, Lichen clawed for the knife on his hip but apparently he thought better of the notion and held his hands out from his sides. "You had no call to do that."

"It's what happens when you insult folks."

"Calling you an Injun lover was an insult? I'd say it fits any gent who's lived with them."

"It's not what you say," Fargo set him straight. "It's how you say it." He left them to ponder that and went to the other fire. Senator Keever was lighting a pipe. Gerty was doodling in the dirt with a stick. "Mind if I join you?"

"I do," Gerty said without looking up.

The senator chuckled. "Pay no attention to her. She thinks she can boss people around as she likes."

"Usually I can," Gerty said. "But not him. He never does anything I want him to. He's as contrary as a mule."

"When will you get it through your head that you can't go around telling people what to do?"

"You do."

Keever lowered his pipe. "That's not quite true. In my capacity as a senator it might seem that way, but the only people who jump at my commands are my personal staff."

"You boss all kinds of people. I've seen you," Gerty persisted, still without looking up from her doodle. "You boss Rebecca around all the time."

For the first time since Fargo met them, Keever showed a real flash of anger.

"She's your mother and you will address her as such."

"She's not my real mother. I only call her that because you pay me to."

Fargo wasn't sure he'd heard right. "He pays you?"

Gerty glanced at him, deviltry on her face. "He pays me. Five dollars extra on my allowance. He has ever since I found out about my real mother."

Senator Keever was pink in the cheeks. "Pay her no heed. She constantly forgets her station in life."

Gerty laughed. "Father explained it to me once. How we all have our place. How it doesn't do when those who are lower act as if they are higher. Like Rebecca."

"I'm warning you," Senator Keever said.

Bestowing her sweetest smile on him, Gerty replied, "Certainly, Father. Whatever you say, Father. I will always do as you wish, Father."

"You can be a trial, little one."

"I'm thirteen, Father. I'm not little anymore. But I'll try harder to be as you want me to be. I won't talk unless I'm spoken to. I'll eat all my vegetables. I'll say my prayers before bedtime. Cross my heart and hope to die."

Senator Keever nodded. "That's better."

"How does the rest of that go?" Gerty said, tapping her chin. "Oh. Now I remember." She quoted the rhyme. "Cross my heart and hope to die, stick a needle in my mother's eyes." She paused. "Or should I change that to stepmother?"

Keever rose and regarded her as he might a new form of insect. "You are vicious beyond your years, daughter."

Again Gerty smiled ever-so-sweetly. "I have you to thank for that, don't I, Father?"

The senator made for their tent.

Laughing, Gerty winked at Fargo. "Aren't I the luckiest girl alive? To have a loving father like him and a doting mother like Rebecca?"

Fargo shook his head in disgust. "What the hell is wrong with you?"

Gerty clasped a hand to her mouth in mock shock. "Oh my. Such language. But that's all right. You're so wonderfully dumb, I forgive you."

"You didn't answer me."

Gerty sighed and set down the stick. "You're trying to figure me out, is that it? Would you like me to help you? I'll give you a hint as to what I'm truly like." She pointed at the dirt.

Fargo moved closer so he could see. "How is that a hint?"

"Silly man. That's me."

Fargo looked at her and then at the dirt again. She hadn't been doodling. She'd drawn a remarkable likeness—of a rattlesnake.

6

Finding a buffalo herd wasn't that easy. Most of the buffalo were well to the south at that time of year, although here and there small herds could be found if one looked long enough and hard enough.

"Where the hell are they?" Lichen groused. He had been doing a lot of grousing since they started out shortly after daybreak.

"We'll find some," Lem Owen said.

"We better," Senator Keever declared. "I'm paying good money. I expect results."

Fargo kept his eyes fixed on the ground, seeking fresh sign.

"I have an idea," the senator said. "Let's split up. We're bound to find them that much sooner."

"No." Fargo was thinking of the Sioux.

"What do you say, Mr. Owen? You have almost as much experience as Mr. Fargo."

"He's right. It's safer if we stick together. Killing a buff is fine and dandy but not if it gets you scalped by savages."

"I daresay the two of you are a disappointment," Keever told them. "I was under the impression frontiersmen are bold and reckless."

"Only the dead ones," Owen said.

The country was becoming increasingly broken by hills, ridges of rock, and stone outcroppings that towered like gigantic tombstones against a backdrop of hazy blue sky.

Senator Keever noticed. "By the way, when do we reach the Black Hills?"

"You've been in them for a day and a half now," Fargo enlightened him.

"Finally!" Keever grinned and excitedly rubbed his hands. "I can see that trophy on my wall now."

Fargo didn't ask him which one. Then the Ovaro nickered, and he looked up to behold the object of their quest in the form of an old bull not fifty yards away. Head high, it sniffed the air to get their scent.

"I'll be switched," Owen blurted.

Senator Keever had been gazing to the south but now he looked in the direction they were looking and exclaimed, "I knew it! I knew God wouldn't let me down." He bent and yanked his rifle from the saddle scabbard. "Move aside, gentlemen. I'm not about to let an opportunity like this pass by."

"Senator, wait," Fargo said, but Keever did no such thing. He spurred his horse toward the bull.

"That jackass sure is trying to get himself killed," Owen remarked.

Fargo used his spurs. But the Ovaro couldn't overtake the senator's mount, not in the short distance they had to cover. He saw Keever jerk the rifle up and shouted, "Don't do it!"

The rifle boomed.

The buffalo whirled. Raising puffs of dust, it raced into a wash and was out of sight.

"After him, men!" Keever bellowed, giving chase. "I'm sure I wounded it. We can't let it get away!"

"Damn you." Fargo galloped after him.

Owen and Lichen came on quickly, Owen bellowing, "That's not the one you want, Senator! That's not the one you want!"

Which made no sense to Fargo. Keever was out to shoot a buffalo.

What difference did it make which one? Now the fool

was charging into the wash with no thought to his safety or that of his mount.

Fargo cursed all idiots, and Easterners. The smart thing to do was to let the bull run off and track it at their leisure. But no. All Keever could think of was how the head would look on his wall.

"My trophy room is the envy of Washington," the senator had confided a few days ago. "Two presidents have come to see it. So has nearly everyone of influence. You should hear how many say they wish they had trophies of their own. But they say their wives would object. Or their constituents would be offended. Or they're just too cowardly to stalk and face a wild beast."

Fargo had pointed out that it wasn't yellow to fight shy of grizzlies and buffalo.

"I say different. I say a man is measured by his deeds."

Now the great huntsman, as Keever liked to call himself, was winding along the serpentine bottom of the wash, whooping and waving his Whitworth like a damned lunatic.

Fargo would as soon shoot him.

A bend appeared, and Senator Keever went around it on the fly.

A piercing squeal told Fargo that which he dreaded had happened. He lashed the Ovaro. The senator's life span could be measured in seconds unless he got to him quickly.

The buffalo had run as far as it was going to, and turned at bay. When the senator came galloping around the bend, the bull lowered its head and slammed broadside into his horse. The squeal Fargo heard was its cry of pain as the bull buried its horns deep. Now the horse was on its side, whinnying and kicking, while Keever sought to free his pinned leg and scamper to safety.

But the bull wasn't done. It loomed over them, a shaggy juggernaut bent on ripping and rending.

Fargo drew rein and whipped the Henry to his shoulder.

He fired, worked the lever, fired again. He went for the head because that was all he had to shoot at; the bull was facing him. But as every plainsman worth his buckskins already knew, shooting a buffalo in the head was a waste of lead. It was like shooting a wall or a boulder. Slugs had no more effect than gnats, except to make the bull mad.

With a tremendous bellow of pure rage, the buffalo bounded around the thrashing horse and came after Fargo and the Ovaro. Wheeling the stallion, Fargo used his spurs once more. He was barely a buckboard's length ahead of the bull as he raced around the bend—and almost collided with Owen and Lichen, who were coming the other way. They both jerked on their reins and brought their mounts to a sliding stop. Which suited the bull just fine. Snorting, it veered at Owen's dun but the dun was halfway up the wash in a few bounds.

Fargo had slowed to see if either of them went down, and now the bull was almost on top of him. He reined aside with inches to spare. The bull kept on going and was lost to view around the next bend.

"Son of a bitch," Lichen fumed.

Owen had already reined back down. "Where did the senator get to? He nearly got me killed."

Keever was still pinned by his horse, which had stopped thrashing and lay still in a spreading pool of scarlet. "Help me," he requested, pushing in vain against the saddle.

"You damned jackass. That was a harebrained stunt you just pulled," Fargo said bluntly. "The next time you do anything like this, you can find yourself another guide." He went to dismount.

"Hold on," Owen said. "It would serve the sorry cuss right if we left him there a while. Say, five or six hours."

Propped on his elbows, Keever regarded them in disbelief. "What is this? I told you I want a buffalo head for my trophy room. What did you expect me to do? Let it get away?"

"I expect you to do what I tell you," Fargo said. "There's a safe way to hunt and there's a dead way to hunt and you didn't pick the safe way."

"Honestly. You forget who you're speaking to. I've shot as much game as either of you. So don't treat me as if I'm still in diapers."

"Then don't act as if you are," Owen said.

Fargo climbed down. He was still mad but he had cooled enough to say calmly, "You've cost us a good horse, Senator, and we don't have many to spare."

"It wasn't as if I planned it. Good Lord, man. Stop making a mountain out of a molehill and get me out from under this thing."

Fargo and Owen tried but they couldn't lift the saddle high enough. They were forced to use a rope, just as they had with the black bear. Fargo climbed on the Ovaro, deftly tossed a loop over the bay's saddle horn, then had the stallion slowly walk backward. Owen was ready, and the instant the saddle rose high enough, he pulled the senator out from under it and helped him to stand.

"At last," Keever said gruffly. He brushed at his expensive clothes and picked pieces of grass from a sleeve. "Which one of you will let me ride his horse to camp?"

"You can ride double with me if you like," Owen offered.

"What about my saddle?"

"Lichen will bring it back with him." Owen chuckled and winked at Fargo. "Damn. Here I am, doing your work. I would make as good a top dog as you."

"We've been all through that," Fargo reminded him.

Owen rubbed his jaw. "That we have. Still, I should get a raise, all the extra work I do."

The senator was smoothing his hair. "I can remedy that. From here on out I'll pay you a third more than you have been getting."

"You sure are generous," Owen said sarcastically.

"You know what I'm after. You want generous? Find it for me."

"Find what?" Fargo asked.

"How many times must I repeat myself? I want a buffalo and a grizzly to add to my trophies and make this trek worthwhile."

They rode slowly. Owen was in a talkative mood and went on about the weather and how hard it was proving to find buffalo and how maybe they should save shooting a buff for last and instead penetrate deeper into the Black Hills after a griz.

"These hills are special to the Sioux," Fargo brought up.

"Oh posh," Senator Keever said. "We have only seen a few Indians since we crossed the Mississippi River. I was led to believe the plains are crawling with them."

Owen pointed. "There's some for you."

Six warriors on horseback were far off to the northwest, heading north. Their backs were to them.

"Sioux, you think?" the senator asked.

Fargo swung down and instructed them to do the same. Owen and Lichen quickly complied but Keever stayed on.

"Here you go again. Making a fuss when they don't even see us."

Owen grabbed the senator's leg and yanked, nearly unhorsing him. "Get off, you simpleton."

"I am growing severely weary of your insults," Keever said. But he dismounted.

Fargo kept one hand on the Henry. It bothered him, the one warrior before and now these six. A village must be near, in which case they should pack everything up and get the hell out of there. He mentioned it to Keever.

"Give up because we've seen a few Indians? Why, I'd be the laughingstock of the Senate."

"There are worse things," Owen said. "Like being the laughingstock of the cemetery."

Fargo began to wonder why Keever put up with Owen's constant prodding. But he put it from his mind. He had something more important to think about: the Sioux. "I'm going to follow them," he announced.

"You're loco."

"I don't see the point," the senator asked. "Let them go their way and we'll go ours."

"I'll shadow them and find out if their village is nearby," Fargo explained. "If it is, we're lighting a shuck whether you like it or not." He forked leather. The six warriors were almost out of sight. "Take Keever back," he directed Owen, "and keep your eyes skinned."

Owen grinned. "Says the gent out to part company with his hair."

The senator cleared his throat. "I really must protest. You're taking a rash risk. We've avoided them so far and we can keep on doing so if we use our heads."

"I am using mine." Fargo gigged the Ovaro. He stayed at a walk. The warriors were in no hurry and he wasn't anxious to get any closer than he already was. Half an hour crawled by, then an hour. The six were barely visible. The terrain became hillier and more broken, typical of the Black Hills, or *Paha Sapa*, as the Sioux called them. To the Sioux they were sacred.

Fargo had lived with the Sioux once. They referred to themselves as the Lakotas, and were, in fact, made up of seven bands, among them the Hunkpapa, Miniconjou, and the Oglala.

Unlike the Shoshones and Flatheads, who were friendly to whites, the Lakotas resented white intrusion into their lands and killed most every white they came across.

Fargo had been an exception.

He didn't blame them for protecting their land. Hell, he hated the advance of civilization as much as they did. To him it meant the loss of the open prairie and the high country he loved to roam.

The warriors were out of sight.

A tap of his spurs and Fargo brought the stallion to a canter. He expected to spot them almost immediately. But he covered a quarter of a mile, and no Sioux. Puzzled, he flicked his reins and had the Ovaro trot for half a mile, with the same result.

Something wasn't right. Fargo slowed to a walk. He didn't think they had seen him, but then again, all it would take was one warrior with eyes as sharp as a hawk's to look back at just the right moment.

His skin prickling, Fargo placed his hand on his Colt. He would go on a little ways yet, and if he didn't spot them, turn back.

The last Fargo saw of the six, they were winding between a pair of wooded hills. Both hills were about the same size and shape, and reminded him of a woman's breasts. He grinned at the notion, and thought of Rebecca Keever, of her full bosom and winsome figure.

The next moment Fargo lost his grin when the trees to his right and the trees to his left disgorged shrieking warriors brandishing lances and notching arrows to sinew strings.

He had ridden into a trap.

7

The Ovaro burst into motion at a jab of Fargo's spurs. The warriors were on both sides and slightly behind him; if he tried to go back the way he came, they would cut him off. So he headed deeper into the hills, the Lakota hard in pursuit.

Fargo could have shot a few. He could have jerked the Henry from the scabbard and banged away before they came within arrow range. But it would cost him precious seconds.

There was also the fact that while the Sioux, on rare occasion, would let a white man live, they killed anyone, white or red, who killed a Sioux.

Fargo rode for his life. The ground between the hills was open and he could hold to a gallop. But soon he came to thick woods where the slightest mistake on his part or a misstep by the Ovaro would reap calamity. Fortunately, the Ovaro was sure-footed and quick-hoofed, and avoided obstacles like downed logs and boulders with an alacrity few horses could match.

It was partly why Fargo never lacked for confidence in the stallion. It had saved his hide countless times. He expected that this time would be no different, that the Ovaro's exceptional stamina would enable him to widen his lead to where the warriors had no chance of catching him. He glanced back, and smiled. He was gaining.

Fargo faced around. Too late, he saw a low limb. He ducked, or tried to, but the limb struck him full across the chest. Pain ripped through him as he was swept bodily from the saddle and crashed to earth. He landed on his back, his head swimming. The breath had been knocked out of him, and it was all he could do to rise on his elbows in a vain bid to get up. He got his hands under him but he couldn't muster the strength to stand.

Then Fargo's head cleared and he saw the Ovaro twenty yards away, looking back at him. "Here, boy," he croaked. Again he tried to stand. This time he made it to his knees but his chest was hurting so bad, he had to grit his teeth against the agony.

Hooves drummed, approaching swiftly.

Fargo pushed up off the ground. He swayed. He took a faltering step. His body wouldn't do what he wanted it to. Concentrating, he started to walk, but oh-so-slow.

The hooves became thunder.

Fargo turned and dropped a hand to his Colt. He figured the warriors would turn him into a porcupine but not until after he took more than a few with him. One was already in midair. A shoulder slammed into his chest, into the same spot the limb had caught him. He was bowled over and wound up on his back with the warrior on top, the warrior's legs pinning his arms. He tried to rise but couldn't. He was helpless, completely, totally helpless.

The warrior grinned and raised a gleaming knife on high.

Fargo tensed. He had always known it would end like this someday. He'd tempted the jaws of fate again and again, and now those jaws were closing. He held no regrets, though. He'd lived a good life. Maybe not good by the standards of some, but good by his own reckoning. All the women, the whiskey, the cards, had been the spice that gave his life taste.

The knife gleamed in the sunlight.

That was when a swarthy arm flicked out and a swarthy hand gripped the wrist of the knife-wielder.

"*Heyah*." It was Lakota for "No."

The warrior with the knife wasn't happy. "Why not?" he demanded, adding, "*Anapo*." He wanted to count coup.

"I know this white-eye."

Fargo found his breath and said quietly, "*Unshimalam ye oyate*."

The warrior about to stab him showed surprise at hearing his own tongue from white lips. He had lived maybe twenty winters, and wore his long hair loose. "Why should I spare you? You are my enemy."

"I have lived with the Lakotas. I have shared their lodges." Fargo glanced at the other warrior, the one who had stopped the knife from being buried in his body. "My heart is happy to see you again, Four Horns."

"It should be." Four Horns grinned. He was in his forties, his features typical of his people: a high forehead, high cheekbones, a long nose, and square jaw. He wore his hair in braids.

The warrior on Fargo's chest still hadn't lowered the knife.

"What will it be, One Feather?" Four Horns demanded. "Kill him or get off him. But if you kill him we are no longer friends."

One Feather frowned. He glared at Fargo, then slid the knife into a fringed sheath. "I spare you, white-eye. But not because I want to. But for Four Horns." He stood and stepped back.

The rest of the warriors were still on their mounts, some staring at Fargo in open hostility.

Four Horns offered his hand. "It has been almost five winters since I saw you last, He Who Walks Many Trails."

"*Pila mita*." Fargo let himself be pulled to his feet. He still had the Colt but if he so much as touched it, he would be dead before he got off a shot.

"Why are you in the land of the Lakotas?"

"Hunting," Fargo answered honestly. He touched a hand to his chest, and winced.

Four Horns cocked his head. "Why come here to hunt when there is so much game elsewhere? Is it worth risking your hair for meat?"

"I happened to be passing through," Fargo lied. He didn't dare tell them the truth. They would go after the senator's party.

Four Horns turned to the warriors on horseback. He spoke so fast that Fargo had trouble following what he said but it was something to the effect that Fargo was his friend and he would be grateful if they didn't kill him.

"It is wrong to spare a white-eye," One Feather said. "They always bring trouble."

"I think highly of the Lakotas," Fargo said in his own defense. "I want to be their friend."

"You lie. Whites want us dead."

Four Horns said, "I tell you I have shared meat with him. He always speaks with a straight tongue."

That was about as high a compliment a Sioux warrior could pay someone. Fargo was grateful. Even more so when One Feather grunted in disgust and walked over to his horse.

"One Feather is young yet," Four Horns said with a tinge of sadness. "All he thinks of is counting coup."

"Too many on both sides think only of killing," Fargo agreed.

"Let us sit and talk."

Four Horns moved a stone's throw from his friends and sank down cross-legged in the grass. Folding his arms, he smiled warmly. "If I had my pipe we could smoke."

"*Cola*," Fargo said.

"Yes, I am your friend. As your friend I warn you to get on your horse and leave the Black Hills. There are Lakota everywhere and more are coming."

"Why?" Fargo asked. It was normal for the bands to pay

the hills a visit but not for all of them to converge at the same time. "Are the Lakota making great medicine? Is there a council of war?" For some time there had been rumors that the bands were going to gather together in a concerted push to drive the white man out. Fargo didn't doubt that if it ever came to pass, blood would flow in rivers.

"You have not heard?"

"I have been in the white man's lands far to the south. I have not heard anything about my Lakota brothers."

Four Horns smiled happily. "It is glorious, my friend. A white buffalo has been born."

Fargo's interest was piqued. To many tribes, white buffalo were special. They were living symbols of hope and unity. The Indians held them in the same high regard as the white man held, say, his church or his Bible. "Where is this animal?"

"Here." Four Horns gestured at the hills. "Exactly where, I will not say. We kept it a secret. I hope I do not hurt your feelings by not telling you."

"I understand."

"It has been many winters since a white buffalo was among us. It is why the bands gather. Not one or two or three but all seven. All the warriors, all the leaders."

That meant thousands of Sioux, Fargo realized.

"The Arapaho have asked to see the white buffalo. The Cheyenne, as well. It will bring many of the tribes together."

"It is good fortune for you," Fargo told him.

"Little Face said the same words."

Fargo frowned. Little Face was what whites would call a medicine man, or shaman. Fargo had met him a few times and didn't like him for the simple reason Little Face was a bigot. Just as there were whites who hated the red man because the red man wasn't white, so were there red men who hated the white man because the white man wasn't red. "I am glad you are sitting there and not Little Face."

Four Horns' eyes sparkled with humor. "He is still mad at you over the white woman."

Fargo remembered. The Sioux had attacked a wagon train. They killed a score of whites and took a white woman hostage. Little Face wanted her for himself but Fargo persuaded the council to let her go back to her own kind. "He sure does hold a hate."

"Little Face hates you with all he is. Were you his prisoner he would stake you out and skin you."

Fargo glanced at the other warriors. One Feather was fingering his knife. "I ask only to go my way in peace."

"If I help you, you must agree to leave our land."

Fargo had no objections and he doubted Senator Keever would, either, when Keever learned about the gathering of the bands. "You have my word."

Four Horns smiled and put a hand on Fargo's shoulder. "I have missed you, my brother. You are one of the few whites who looks at me and sees a man and not the color of my skin."

"*Cola*," Fargo said warmly.

Four Horns grunted, and stood. Fargo followed his example and they walked over to where the other warriors waited.

One Feather pointed at Fargo. "I still want to kill this one. He should not be in the *Paha Sapa*."

"*Heyah*," Four Horns said. He gripped the Ovaro's reins and placed them in Fargo's hand. "Go now, He Who Walks Many Trails. And may it be many moons before we see each other again."

Fargo didn't linger. One Feather and some of the others were too outright eager to kill him. They were under no obligation to do as Four Horns wanted, and might change their minds at any moment. "*Pila mita*."

"Go," Four Horns urged. Fargo touched his hat brim and got the hell out of there. But he had gone only a short way when a war whoop warned him he was far from safe.

One Feather and two other young warriors were after him.

Once again Fargo resorted to his spurs. He deliberately rode to the southwest; the camp was to the southeast.

One Feather was yipping up a storm.

Fargo had met young warriors like him before. Eager to prove themselves, they counted coup every chance they got. He could hardly blame them, since counting coup was considered not only a test of a warrior's courage but a mark of leadership.

The three Sioux came on fast but the Ovaro was faster. Bit by bit the stallion pulled ahead until it was apparent to the three that they stood no chance whatsoever of catching him. Howling their fury and exasperation, they drew rein.

Fargo looked back, smiled, and waved. "That should rub it in."

One Feather howled and shook his fist.

Chuckling, Fargo kept on to the southwest. Half an hour later he brought the sweat-caked stallion to a stop. Taking off his hat, he wearily mopped his brow with his sleeve.

Fargo reckoned he could safely swing to the east toward camp, but stick figures on the horizon changed his mind. Four Horns hadn't been kidding when he said there were Lakota everywhere.

Bending low, Fargo gigged the Ovaro. He figured it would take him two to three hours to get back. Longer, if he ran into a lot of Sioux.

Fate was in a fickle mood. Again and again he spotted riders in the distance and had to seek cover or veer in a direction he didn't want to go to avoid being spotted.

It began to look as if it would be sunset before Fargo rejoined Keever's party.

He grew weary of the cat and mouse. His nerves were stretched to where a light patter brought him around with his Colt out and level, but it was only a coyote he had spooked, now slinking off.

By mere chance Fargo came on a spring. Nestled in the lee of a thickly wooded hill, it was an ideal spot to rest.

Fargo dismounted and let the Ovaro drink. Dropping onto his belly, he took off his hat and dipped his face in the wonderfully cool water. He had been sweltering, but in no time he was cool and refreshed and content.

Rolling onto his back, Fargo closed his eyes. A nap would do him good but he needed to warn the senator. He would lie there a few minutes and be on his way.

The Ovaro stamped a hoof.

With a start, Fargo sat up. He had dozed off. A glance at the sun assured him it had only been for a few minutes. Nevertheless, it was the sort of blunder a greenhorn made.

"Damn me for a yack," Fargo said out loud, and jammed his hat back on. He sighed and went to stand. Only then did he notice that the Ovaro was looking at something behind him.

It occurred to Fargo that he had made two blunders, not one. He started to turn but froze when the sharp tip of a knife jabbed him between the shoulder blades.

"Move and I kill you."

8

Fargo moved anyway; he turned his head in surprise. First, that someone had snuck up on him without him hearing. Second, that the "someone" holding a knife to his back was female.

She had raven hair and ink for eyes, fine full lips, and a bosom that strained against a doeskin dress. Her hourglass figure would be the envy of any woman, white or red. She was as gorgeous a female as Fargo ever set eyes on, and that was saying a lot. She was also Sioux.

There was nothing gorgeous about the steel blade she had gouged against Fargo's back. Just as there was nothing friendly about the hard glint in her dark eyes.

"Your name must be Sweet Flower."

The woman jerked back as if he had slapped her. She saw his smile and those full lips started to curl but she caught herself and jabbed him with the knife, harder than before.

"You speak the Lakota tongue."

"I am a friend to your people. My heart is one with Four Horns. He sits high in the councils of the Miniconjou."

"I am an Oglala," the young woman said, and frowned. "I do not want you to talk. I must decide what to do with you."

Fargo kept on smiling. "I know what I would like to do." To make sure she got the point, he roved his gaze from the crown of her lustrous hair to the tips of her moccasin-clad feet, with pauses where needed.

"You are too bold."

"How should I call you?" Fargo asked.

"Sweet Flower will do."

Fargo chuckled and started to turn but the knife convinced him not to. "You can take that away. I would never hurt anyone so lovely."

"You are much too bold. I should call for help. Warriors would come and then we would see how bold you are."

Fargo noticed that she didn't holler. "Your village is near?"

"Yes."

Something told Fargo she was lying. "I will let you go back, pretty Sweet Flower, and I will be on my way."

"You will *let* me?" she said, and raised the knife a few inches. "You are my captive. I am not yours."

"You are a beautiful dove and a dove should never be in a cage." Fargo winked, and moved. A twist of his body, a flick of his hand, and the deed was done; he held the knife and her hand was empty.

Sweet Flower gasped and poised for flight.

"Here." Fargo reversed his grip and placed the hilt in her palm. "I told you I would never harm you."

Her confusion was obvious. She looked at the knife and she looked at him and then she moved a few yards away and squatted. "I do not know what to think about you."

"I am your friend if you want me to be." Fargo knelt, cupped water, and sipped. He deliberately ignored her. When he was done drinking he took off his hat and splashed water on his neck and face.

"Does your hair itch?"

Fargo reached up and scratched his head. "No. Does yours?"

Lilting laughter rippled from her silken throat. "Not there," Sweet Flower said, and rubbed her chin. "The hair on your face. My people do not have hair there. Our warriors are not as hairy as you whites."

"Not all white men have a lot of hair," Fargo enlightened her.

"Do white women like those who do? I do not know if I would like it."

"For some white women, hair is all they think about," Fargo said with a straight face. "Others like their men as smooth as a baby's bottom."

Sweet Flower laughed again. "Why do you keep doing that?"

"What? Growing hair?"

"You should be a Heyoka. You are funny."

Fargo was familiar with the contraries, who did everything backward. To whites it seemed silly if not downright stupid. But to the Lakotas, the Heyokas were their clowns, men and women who brought laughter and delight into their lives. "I thank you for the compliment."

"Tell me about yourself." Fargo kept it short. His Indian name, some of the places he had been, some of the tribes he had lived with or fought against.

"You have been to the land of the Comanches? I have heard of them from my grandfather. He says that when they ride a horse, the horse and the Comanche are one."

"He speaks with a straight tongue."

"Tell me. Of all the tribes you have known, who are the best fighters?"

Fargo didn't hesitate. Nearly every tribe took pride in the fighting prowess of its warriors. But there was one that, in his estimation, was head and shoulders above the rest when it came to killing their enemies. "The Apaches."

"I have heard of them too. The People of the Woods, they call themselves. Are they truly so fierce?"

"To kill without being killed is the law they live by. Were there ten thousand of them, they would have all the land from the Muddy River to the western sea."

"Are they handsome?"

"They are short and heavy and as hairy as bears," Fargo exaggerated. "They itch a lot and are always scratching." He was rewarded with more merriment.

"You talk with two tongues now. I have been told Apache men are handsome. Not as handsome as Lakota men. But a woman would not complain if she were taken by them."

"Only a female would say a thing like that." Fargo leaned back. He should be on his way to warn the senator. But it would help to know exactly how near her people were.

"You are fond of women. I can tell. I see the hunger in your eyes when you look at me."

"Any man would look at you with hunger," Fargo piled on the praise. "You must have a husband. Lakota men would not let such beauty be wasted."

"I lived in the lodge of Left Handed Buffalo for a winter but he was not nice to me. He tried to give me away but I went back to live with my mother and father." Sweet Flower paused. "Do you have a woman?"

"Not in the past, not now, not ever," Fargo declared. He caught movement off in the trees and stiffened but it was only her pony, tied to a tree and grazing. "What if your people come along? Will you get in trouble talking to me?"

She answered without thinking. "They do not know where I am. I wanted to go for a ride and my horse brought me here. She must have smelled the water."

"So it is just the two of us." Fargo pushed his hat back, and grinned.

"Much, much too bold." Sweet Flower stood. "I must go. But if you were to be here tomorrow I would come and talk to you again."

"I will try." Fargo was half serious. He would very much like the pleasure of her company, but not just to talk. He watched her sway off and reflected that when it came to jiggling deliciously, women everywhere were the same. With a sigh he climbed on the Ovaro.

About two hours of daylight were left. Fargo rode hard but warily. He saw no Sioux, and it was with relief that he came within sight of camp, and a crackling fire.

"Where have you been?" Senator Keever demanded the moment Fargo came to a stop. "Mr. Owen about had me convinced the savages had caught you and scalped you."

"They almost did," Fargo acknowledged. Wearily dismounting, he began to strip the Ovaro.

Most of the others gathered around.

"I'm glad you're back safe," Rebecca said.

Gerty scrunched up her face. "I'm not. I wanted the Indians to get you and scalp you so you can't be mean to me anymore."

"Gertrude! That's no way to talk."

"Oh, hush," Keever snapped at his wife. "She's only speaking her mind. He's a grown man. He can take it."

Owen nudged Lichen with an elbow and said in mock delight, "We sure are glad you made it. I've been a bundle of worry. I couldn't eat. I couldn't drink. It was plumb awful."

Lichen cackled.

They didn't know how close they came to being pistol-whipped. Instead, Fargo said loud enough for all to hear, "I want everyone to gather around in about ten minutes." That would give him time to strip the Ovaro and wet his throat. "I have something important to say."

"You're leaving us?" Gerty teased.

"No. I sold you to the Sioux."

"Father!" she squealed. "Did you hear him? Did you hear how mean he is to me?"

"Yes, daughter, I did. That was uncalled for, sir. You should set a better example."

"She's your brat, not mine. The only things she'd learn from me is how to play poker, drink red-eye, and make the acquaintance of saloon doves."

"That will be quite enough of that kind of talk," Senator

Keever said indignantly. "Need I remind you in whose employ you are? I told you at the outset that you and the other men must watch your tongues around my daughter and my wife."

Fargo noticed that he put his daughter first. Hunkering, he poured coffee into his battered tin cup, sat back, and let the hot liquid trickle down his dry throat. Senator Keever and Gerty went to their tent. The other men milled idly about, talking and joking.

"Mind if I join you?" Rebecca squatted across from him, her forearms across her knees. "I meant what I said. I really am glad you made it back safe."

Fargo sipped more coffee. She had something on her mind, he could tell, and she would get to it in her own good time.

"You're the only one I can talk to. If that sounds strange, it's only because my so-called husband doesn't care what I think or how I feel about things. As for Gerty—" Rebecca shrugged.

"She would make fine bear bait."

Rebecca snorted, then covered her nose and mouth with her hand. "You can be awful at times."

"Lady, you don't know the half of it."

"I wish I could be like you. I wish I had your courage. I've always been a mouse, myself. Too timid for my own good. I let myself be talked into things I shouldn't."

"Such as being here," Fargo guessed.

"Such as being married." Rebecca glanced at the tent and lowered her voice. "You see, our marriage isn't quite what you think. Oh, I took the vows, and I go where he goes and do what he wants me to do. But only because he's paying me."

"I must have missed something."

"You know that his first wife died in childbirth. He blames it on her consumption. She became so weak she didn't want to live. But that's only part of it. She wasn't tired of living. She was tired of *him*!"

"How do you know?"

"I was one of the nurses who attended her. He didn't tell you that, did he? Or that while his wife lay wasting away in her hospital bed, he was playing the satyr with every nurse on my floor."

Fargo wondered why she was telling him this. "Including you?"

"No. Oh, he tried. He spouted the same honey-tongued lies about how beautiful I was and how he would love to take me out and wouldn't it be grand if we went up to his house after?" Rebecca didn't hide her disgust. "But I told him he should be ashamed. That what he was doing was despicable. And do you know what he did? He laughed and offered me money to be his new wife."

"Maybe it was his way of getting up your dress."

"No. He was serious. He offered to pay me two thousand dollars a year plus a thousand extra if I stick out the terms of the contract he had a lawyer draw up. I know, I know. You don't understand. You're going to say I'm crazy. But you haven't heard the whole story yet."

"My ears work fine."

"Eh? Oh." Rebecca nervously laughed. "The good senator is a pillar of Congress. All Fulton cares about is power. He wants to stay in office another twenty years. To do that, he has to be reelected, and to be reelected he has to convince the good folks back home that he's a paragon of virtue and worthy of their support."

"You're saying he isn't."

Rebecca wrung her hands in her lap. "He's the worst womanizer who ever lived. His wife despised him for it. She was thinking of divorcing him. Then she became pregnant. She didn't want a baby. She hated the idea. But he insisted she go through with it. And look at what it got her."

"I still don't see where you come in."

Tears filled Rebecca's eyes but she blinked and wiped at her face with a sleeve. "I was a hard-working nurse who barely made ends meet. Two thousand dollars a year was a lot of money to me. I agreed, and he's been putting the money in my bank account ever since. His only condition was that I never, ever tell anyone his secret. Which I never have until now."

Fargo supposed he should feel flattered.

"I had conditions of my own," Rebecca hastily went on. "I agreed to play his wife but only so long as he didn't bring any of his tarts back home with him." She stopped, and bit her lower lip. "My other condition was that he couldn't lay a hand on me. I'm not his and never will be. Not that way."

"Is there a point to all this?"

"Yes." Rebecca looked him in the eyes and said so softly he barely heard her, "I haven't been with a man in thirteen years and I can't take it anymore. I want you to make love to me."

9

Skye Fargo thought he had seen it all and heard it all. He thought he had stopped being surprised by the loco things people did. But he was wrong. "You haven't slept with a man in thirteen *years*?"

"I didn't say that, exactly," Rebecca said.

"Then what the hell did you say?"

"I said I haven't *been* with another man. I didn't say I haven't slept with a few."

Fargo almost laughed in her face. Leave it to a female to split hairs. "How is that different?"

"When a woman says she's been with a man, it means it was more than just physical. Oh, I've been attracted to a few, like I am to you. But I've only ever slept with them and nothing more. Understand?"

No, Fargo didn't. But if she wanted to go on kidding herself, that was fine by him. He was about to suggest they get together later when Senator Keever and Gerty came out of their tent. Owen and Lichen and the rest of the men took that as their cue to converge.

"So what is it you wanted to discuss?" the senator asked.

Fargo had been thinking about it on the ride back and there was only one thing to do. "We're packing up and heading for civilization in the morning. I want everyone up by six so we can be on our way by seven."

Keever half grinned. "Is this some kind of joke? I came to

the Black Hills to hunt and I'm not leaving until I have a few more trophies."

"If we stay the Sioux will have trophies of their own and one might be your scalp. We're caught smack in the middle of a gathering of the bands, and if we're not real careful, we'll be up to our necks in warriors out to slit our throats."

Owen appeared to be skeptical. "What's this gathering business? There hasn't been a gathering of all the Sioux in years. What could bring the bands together now?"

"A white buffalo."

Senator Keever and Owen exchanged looks and the senator said, "We're talking about an albino buffalo, correct? There are albino animals all the time. I've seen an albino deer myself. So why are the redskins making such a fuss over this white one?"

"To the Lakotas it's sacred."

"Oh, hogwash. An albino isn't exceptional. I grant you they're rare. But it's a buffalo, for God's sake. A shaggy brute that spends it days grazing and grunting and leaving smelly droppings all over the place. How in the world can even simple savages think it's sacred?"

"A lot of whites think the same about their Bibles, don't they?"

"Be serious, Mr. Fargo. Scripture is the divine word of the Almighty. A white buffalo is a lowly animal, nothing more."

Fargo sighed. "The point is that these hills are crawling with Sioux, and more are showing up every day. It's only a matter of time before some of them spot us. We can't stay."

Some of the men began to talk in hushed tones.

"Now look what you've done." The senator made a dismissive gesture. "*I'm* staying, whether you do or not. And I'll pay every man who stays with me an extra fifty dollars."

"You'll get them killed," Fargo warned.

Owen made a clucking sound. "How about if you let us

be the judge of that? Me, I like the notion of more money. It's only for a week or so. By then the senator will have the trophy he's after and we can head back."

"Exactly right," Keever confirmed.

"I don't know," one of the men spoke up. "The Sioux can be downright vicious. I saw a soldier once that they'd scalped and did things to that would curl your hair."

"Fine," Keever said stiffly. "Leave if you want to. But I'll have no truck with cowards. Don't expect the other half of the pay you're due."

"Don't be so prickly. I didn't say I was leaving. I only said as how the Sioux don't ever show any mercy."

"There are eleven of you. Twelve rifles if you count mine. Thirteen if Mr. Fargo doesn't desert us. That's more than enough to hold any number of savages at bay."

Fargo sighed again. He was beginning to think the senator was the reason the word stupid had been invented. "I said it was a gathering of *all* the bands. There will be thousands of warriors. You and your dozen rifles wouldn't stand a prayer."

Keever turned to Owen. "And you, sir? You have as much experience with these heathens as he does. Do you share his opinion? Should I give up my quest when I'm so close?"

"It will be a cold day in hell before I tuck tail and run from redskins. Oh, we'll have to be on our guard. But our camp isn't anywhere near where they'll set up their villages. They need water, and a lot of it, and plenty of graze for their horses." Owen motioned at the timbered hills that ringed the small valley. "We can hide right under their red noses for as long as you need."

"I thought as much," Keever smugly declared. "There you have it, Mr. Fargo. Stay or go. The choice is yours." He wheeled. "Come, Gerty. We'll wash up for supper. Rebecca, be sure our meal is prepared on time."

Owen and Lichen and the others drifted off, leaving Fargo and Rebecca alone.

"I could have told you how he would react."

Fargo wasn't in the mood to mince words. "He's a jackass. Yet you stayed with him all these years."

"I have over twenty thousand dollars in the bank. How much do you have?"

Fargo made a zero of his thumb and forefinger. "All this money you've saved, was it worth it?"

Rebecca bowed her head and slowly shook it. "No. If I had it to do over again, I wouldn't. Back then I thought money was everything. Now I know better. You can't put a price on happiness."

Fargo stared at their tent. An hour ago he wouldn't have said what he was about to say now. "Do you still want me to do you?"

"What? Oh. I wouldn't put it quite so crudely, but yes. Please. That is, if you want to."

"You wear a dress, don't you?"

"Why do you sound so mad? And why are you agreeing? Because you want to? Or to spite my poor excuse for a husband?"

"Does it matter?" Fargo stretched out his legs. "Wait until him and the brat are asleep and slip out. I'll be waiting, and when I see you, we'll go off into the woods."

"Just the two of us? In the dark?"

"What did you expect? We'd take Owen or one of the others along to stand guard while I poke you?"

"Mad *and* bitter. You have a low tolerance for fools, don't you? I used to before I became one myself."

Rebecca rose and went about cooking stew for her husband and her stepdaughter. Over at the other fire, Lichen was butchering a doe someone had shot while Fargo was gone.

For Fargo's part, he drank coffee and fumed. If it wasn't

for Rebecca, he would light a shuck then and there. He felt a twinge of conscience about Gerty. The girl was the spitting image of her father but she was young yet and didn't know any better. Give her a few years and she might mature. Not that she would live to see old age. Not with an army of Sioux roaming the hills. She wasn't quite old enough to make a good wife so the Lakotas were likely to leave her to die of thirst or hunger. Or maybe, if she was lucky, they'd take her under their wing.

Fargo was on his third cup of coffee when Owen came up to the fire, squatted, and smiled.

"What the hell do you want?"

"The girl is right. You *are* a grump."

"Go to hell. And leave me be."

"I didn't walk over here to swap insults. I wanted to talk to you about the Sioux."

"We've already talked. Maybe you don't recollect, but you persuaded Keever to go on with his hunt. Nice going, buffalo shit for brains."

Owen laughed. "If you were female, I'd swear it was your time of the month."

"If I was a female, I'd swear you were as ugly as sin."

Again Owen laughed but his mirth was forced. "Look, I'm trying to avoid an argument."

"Then you came to the wrong place." Fargo bent toward him and nearly hurled the coffee in his face. "Do you have any idea what you've done? I wasn't exaggerating. In a few days these hills will be swarming with Sioux. More of them than you can imagine."

"I believe you."

"There's no way in hell we can keep hidden. They'll find us, and when they do, every last one of us will be turned into a pincushion."

"I agree."

"Then why didn't you side with me and tell the good senator to leave while he still can?" Fargo shook his head. "I swear. You make no damn sense at all."

"I do to me."

Fargo used a few choice words common in saloons and riverfront dives. "Explain it. Help me to savvy why you're so bent on getting Keever and his family killed."

"I'm not. He is. I'm just doing what he pays me to do." Owen picked up a stick and poked at the flames. "You were hired as their guide. I was hired to advise him. He sat me down and told me exactly what he wants out of this hunt of his and offered me five hundred dollars more than any of the others to make sure he gets his wish."

"This was before we started out?"

"Why do you sound so surprised? Some folks don't think as poorly of me as you do."

"I heard about that dog you dragged to its death."

"Oh, hell. Did you also hear tell it was going around biting horses? Caused one to spook and throw a man."

"So you're a saint now."

"Hell, no. I'm a man doing a job. Same as you. And need I remind you that I saved your hash back at the bluff?"

"You came over just to tell me all this?" God, what Fargo wouldn't give for a whiskey.

"No. I came over to say that if you want to leave, I wouldn't blame you. But I hope you stick around. There's the senator's missus and the girl to think of."

"Now I've heard everything. A saint *and* a heart of gold. Next you'll sprout wings and a halo."

Owen frowned. "You try to be nice to some folks." He stood. "Have it your way. If you want to stay, stay. Just do the rest of us a favor and don't air your bladder about the Sioux." Wheeling, he walked away.

Fargo scratched his head in mild bewilderment. Nothing added up. No one was as they seemed except for Gerty, who looked like a spoiled brat and acted like a spoiled brat. Rebecca played the part of the devoted wife but she was anything but. As for Senator Keever, he was supposed to be a conscientious public servant who never put his own interests first, but that was all he ever did. "It's a damn ridiculous world."

Supper was served. Fargo kept to himself, sipping coffee. After the meal everyone sat around relaxing. Then one by one they turned in. The wind picked up, the stars shifted, and presently everyone was asleep except the two night sentries.

And Fargo. From under his hat brim he watched the tent. He was on his side, his blankets up to his chin. He wondered if Rebecca would go through with it. She stood to lose all the money Keever was paying her if he found out she was playing around on him. But then again, maybe Keever didn't expect her to be a nun, or just didn't care.

Midnight came and went and Fargo had about given it up as a lost cause when the tent flap parted and Rebecca poked her head out. She glanced toward the sentries, then quietly opened the flap and quickly slipped off into the shroud of darkness. A blue silken robe clung to her shapely form like skin.

The sight of it sparked a hunger in Fargo to see more. Rolling onto his back, Fargo mumbled as might a man in his sleep. He saw both sentries over by the horse string, talking. Slowly easing from under his blanket, he slid his saddlebags underneath and fluffed the blanket to lend the illusion he was still under it. Then he removed his hat and placed it where his head would be. It wouldn't stand close scrutiny but he counted on the sentries not paying much attention to the sleepers.

Crabbing backward until he was mantled in ink, Fargo rose and moved beyond the ring of firelight. A shadow separated from deeper shadows, and suddenly Rebecca was clinging to him, her cheek on his shoulder.

"What's the matter?" Fargo whispered.

Rebecca looked up, her face pale and lovely in the starlight. "I was scared. I'm not used to the wilds like you are."

"What were you scared of?"

"I kept hearing sounds."

Fargo heard sounds, too: coyotes, wolves, owls, the bleat of a doe, the snarl of a mountain lion. "It's nothing to worry about."

"I'm not afraid now that you're here." Rebecca hesitated. "But you don't think any Sioux are around, do you?"

"No."

"That's a relief. I don't mind admitting they terrify me. I would hate to end up in some buck's lodge."

To shut her up Fargo kissed her, mashing his lips against hers. She tasted like cherries with a hint of mint. The fragrance she had splashed on was intoxicating.

"Oh, my," Rebecca whispered when he broke for breath. "But must you be so rough?"

Fargo grinned. "You haven't seen anything yet."

10

Fargo went to kiss Rebecca again but she put a hand to his chest and nervously glanced toward camp.

"Not this close. Someone might hear us."

Fargo couldn't see how, since most were asleep. But he took her hand and moved deeper into the dark.

"Let's not go too far," Rebecca whispered. "I want to be able to see the fires."

"Make up your mind."

Sixty feet from their camp, Fargo stopped and pressed Rebecca against a tree. She responded to his kiss but her body was tense and stiff. "What is it now?"

"I'm nervous, I guess." Rebecca looked anxiously about as if she expected a shrieking warrior to come rushing out.

"Relax. We're safe. The Sioux stick close to their lodges at night." Fargo didn't add, "except when war parties go on raids."

"You're sure? What about bears? Or cougars?" Rebecca swallowed. "I don't like these hills at night. I don't like them at all."

Fargo ran his fingers through her hair and placed his other hand on her hip. "Animals won't come this near to fire," he assured her, which wasn't entirely true. A bear might, out of hunger or curiosity. A cougar might, too, if it caught the scent of the horses.

"If you're sure," Rebecca said uncertainly.

Fargo sensed she might change her mind. To prevent that from happening, and to take her mind off what might be lurking in the dark, he cupped her breast while at the same time he slid his other hand between her thighs. She stiffened, and gasped.

Gradually, Rebecca relaxed. Her body molded to his. Her kisses became delicious wellsprings of passion. She sucked on his tongue. She ground against him. Her fingernails scraped his skin.

Fargo relaxed, too. Making love to women had long been a favorite pastime. He would rather poke a willing filly than do just about anything else. He liked it so much that when he went without for more than a week or two, the need built in him until he was fit to explode.

Fargo never could savvy men who swore off women, whatever their reasons. Priests, for instance. Or those who were content with a poke a month, if that. It had surprised him considerably when it dawned on him years back that some men didn't feel the same need he did. For him, the treats a woman offered were a slice of the best the pie of life had to offer, and any gent who didn't care for a taste must not have any taste buds.

Fargo thought of that now as Rebecca continued to warm to their caresses. She pried at his shirt and his belt to get at his pants. He helped, and presently his gun belt was on the ground and his pants were down around his knees. His manhood had become a rigid pole. He shivered when she lightly clasped him and commenced to stroke. He thought he would explode when she cupped him but he was able to contain himself.

Fargo got her robe undone and delved into her charms with ardent zest. He licked her neck. He sucked and nipped an earlobe. He traced the tip of his tongue from her throat to between her breasts and then to a nipple. Inhaling it, he swirled it with his tongue and it became a rigid tack. She groaned when he cupped her other breast. Her hips thrust hard against his member. It was plain her fruit was ripe for the plucking.

Fargo lathered her tummy and stuck his tongue into her navel. He ran his hand from her knees to the junction of her legs. She was burning hot for him. She was wet, too, as he found out when he parted her nether lips with the tip of a finger and ran it over her tiny knob.

Rebecca arched her back. She mewed. Her whole body melted against him in wanton need.

"I've wanted it for so long."

It reminded Fargo of her claim that she hadn't enjoyed much in the way of lovemaking for the past thirteen years. He suspected she wasn't telling the truth, but it was hardly worth bringing up, and definitely not then and there.

Fargo slid a finger into her velvet sheath. He stroked her, and her inner walls rippled. He added a second finger and stroked harder. It aroused her no end; she became an inferno of desire, her lips and hands everywhere.

Fargo drifted on tides of lust until he reached the point where he couldn't wait any longer; he parted her thighs, rubbed the tip of his manhood on her slit, and rammed up into her. Her mouth parted wide and for a moment he thought she would cry out but instead she sank her teeth into his shoulder hard enough for it to hurt.

Fargo devoted his hands to her breasts and his mouth to hers. For a long while he was content to slowly thrust. But as their mutual need mounted and she cooed and squirmed and moaned, he couldn't hold back. He pumped his hips harder and faster and she pumped hers in kind.

The woods blurred. The stars receded. Fargo felt his need to release build and build. Then she gushed and writhed in ecstasy, and it triggered his own explosion. For a while he lost all sense of time, all sense of anything save the addicting pulse of pure pleasure.

The yip of a coyote brought Fargo back to the here and now. He pulled up his pants and strapped on his Colt while she wrapped her robe around herself, and coyly smiled.

"That was wonderful. Thank you."

Fargo grunted.

"Was it good for you? I mean, I don't have a lot of experience so I don't know if I pleased you or not."

"Cut it out," Fargo said.

"I beg your pardon?"

"You're not the poor deprived woman you make yourself out to be. Do me a favor and don't think I'm dumb enough to think you are."

Rebecca frowned. "So you have me all figured out, is that it? I've got news for you. You don't have anyone figured out. Not me. Not Fulton. Not even little Gerty."

"If you say so." That she was so prickly about his remark proved to Fargo he had struck a nerve.

"I know so. Take Fulton, for instance. Do you really think he came all this way to hunt buffalo and bear?"

"Not just any buff or griz. He's after the biggest, the best, to hang on his trophy wall."

"He has you hoodwinked."

Fargo couldn't see how. Senator Keever was paying him good money—paying Owen and Lichen and the others, too—and had spent a lot more on horses and supplies and ammunition. If he wasn't there to hunt, he was putting on a good show. "I'm thickheaded. You need to spell it out."

"I don't know as I will," Rebecca said tartly. "Not after that crack you just made."

"I was only saying."

"I never claimed to be a virginal maiden. I only said I don't get to do it as often as I'd like."

"You're making a fuss over nothing," Fargo said, and knew it was a mistake the moment the words were out of his mouth.

"Oh, really? I trusted you, I confided in you, I gave myself to you, and it's nothing? You don't care how miserable I've been? How very lonely?"

Oh hell, Fargo thought. "You didn't have to marry him. It was your decision, so live with it."

Rebecca straightened and folded her arms. "I would like to go back now, if you don't mind."

"What's stopping you?"

"Alone? In the dark? In these woods? A gentleman like Fulton would never let a lady go by herself."

Fargo was tired of her carping. "What gave you the notion I'm a gentleman? I live in these wilds you dislike so much. I have more in common with a mountain lion than I do the man you married."

"Fulton has a lot of faults but he's always treated me with courtesy. He has a few other traits I admire, too. He's terribly devious, as you'll find out soon enough, to your sorrow."

"There you go again. Dropping hints. If you have something to say, come right out and say it, damn it."

"Temper, temper," Rebecca taunted. "I was thinking about telling you but then you went and insulted me. Now you'll just have to find out on your own. I only hope I'm there to see your face when you discover how you've been tricked."

"Suit yourself." Fargo almost added, "bitch." He turned and strode off and she quickly fell into step beside him.

"Don't walk so fast. I can't keep up." Rebecca added an anxious, "Please, Skye."

Reluctantly, Fargo slowed.

"Listen. I'm sorry. You set me off. But I do like you. Honestly and truly. And I would hate to see you hurt."

Fargo swore. The woman was as fickle as the weather.

"I'm serious. Look. Fulton says you can go if you want. Why not take him up on it? I know Lem tried to talk you out of it but don't listen to him. Your life is more important."

Fargo was about to ask exactly what she meant when it hit him—she had called Owen *Lem*.

"Better yet, leave and take me with you. Gerty, too. This is no place for a woman and a child."

"I tried telling the senator that before we started out, remember?"

"Yes. I heard you. And for your concern, I'm grateful. So why don't we sneak off together? We'll take Gerty. We can do it tomorrow night after everyone is asleep. All you have to do is knock out the men standing watch." Rebecca clutched his wrist and brought him to a stop. "What do you say? Why should we stay and be killed by the savages?" She smiled and rubbed herself against him. "Besides, think of the good times we can have."

Insight smacked Fargo between the eyes. He was being played for a fool. Or, rather, a typical sex-starved male. "So that's what this was."

"I beg your pardon?"

"That tale you told about not sleeping with the senator for thirteen years. And why you were so eager to lure me out here and let me have my way with you." Fargo chuckled. "I've got to hand it to you. You're slick."

Rebecca drew back. "I'm sure I don't know what on earth you're talking about."

"You want out of here. You want out of here so bad, you're willing to do anything. And I do mean *anything*."

In the dark Fargo didn't see her hand until it was too late. She slapped him on the cheek, wheeled, and stalked toward the camp, her entire body as rigid as a board. He laughed lightly and followed but he made no attempt to catch up to her. Now that he was wise to her ruse, he wondered how much of what she had told him was true and how much she made up.

He had a bigger question to answer, namely, should he stay or light a shuck? These people meant nothing to him.

Not any of them. Not now that he knew Rebecca was using him. No, there was nothing holding him.

Except one thing.

Fargo had promised the senator, when Keever hired him, that he would do his best to get them in and out of Sioux country in one piece. To some men that might not mean much. But Fargo never made a promise he couldn't keep, or wouldn't die trying to.

Some folks, Fargo knew, would brand him a sinner. He liked to drink, he liked loose women, he loved to gamble. Flaws of character, they would say. And he would be the first to admit he wasn't the most straitlaced hombre around. But he did have a few scruples, and not breaking his word was one of them. Silly, maybe, but there it was.

And now that Fargo thought about it, he had another reason to stay. Rebecca had hinted her husband was up to something. He would like to know what it was. Fargo had a suspicion. For some time now, rumors had floated around that there was gold in the Black Hills. No one could say how the rumors got started. Normally, that was enough to start a gold rush, as it had in California and elsewhere. But the Black Hills had a deterrent California didn't: the Sioux. A party of whites had snuck in to search for it, and never came out.

Fargo wondered if that was what Keever was after. Presumably, Keever was well-to-do, what with being a senator. But for some folks, there was no such thing as enough money. They always craved more. It was possible the senator had come down with gold fever, and the hunt was a cover so he could scout around for it.

He came to the clearing.

Rebecca was just slipping into the tent. She looked back at him in anger, and jerked the flap shut.

Fargo made sure the night watch had their backs to him, then moved to his blankets. Weariness nipped at him and he closed his eyes.

"It took you long enough."

Fargo looked up. Standing over him was one of the sentries, heavyset, with a bushy mustache and stubble on his chin. Clymer, he thought the man's name was. "What did?"

"Heeding nature's call. I came over here five minutes ago to wake you but you weren't here."

Fargo sat up. "Wake me why?"

"Harris and me keep hearing and seeing something off in the trees. It comes and goes. We don't know what to make of it but we thought you might."

Fargo rose. "I haven't heard anything."

"It's over yonder." Clymer pointed at the far side of the camp, past the horse string. "Come look and give a listen and tell me if you think I'm loco."

"What do you think it is?"

Clymer hesitated. "I'd rather not say. It's best you hear and see for yourself."

"Tell me, damn it."

"Just don't laugh." Clymer took a breath. "I think it's a ghost."

11

It was a good thing Skye Fargo played a lot of poker. A man had to be good at keeping a stone face when he was dealt good cards. It helped in real life when life dealt an idiot or two. Fargo adopted his poker face now as he stared at Clymer. "Did you just say a ghost?"

"I sure did. And before you poke fun, no, I haven't been drinking and neither has Harris. The senator wouldn't let anyone bring liquor, remember?"

That was Fargo's idea. Whiskey and Indian country didn't mix.

"Come see this thing. Maybe you can tell us what it is. Because I've got to admit it has us spooked."

"Lead the way."

Harris was a grubby man who apparently never heard baths were invented. He was pacing beyond the horse string and nervously fingering his rifle. "I saw it again," he said as they came up. "Spookiest thing I ever did see. I'd think I was addlepated if Clymer hadn't seen it too."

"Where is it?" Fargo asked.

Both Harris and Clymer pointed into the forest to the south, and Clymer said, "Just wait. It comes and goes."

"Right now it goes," Harris said.

Fargo cocked his head. The wind stirred the trees, and in the distance a lonesome wolf gave voice to the wavering lament of its breed. He heard nothing else. A minute went by, then a couple. He looked at the two men, and Clymer noticed.

"It's out there, I tell you. Sometimes it takes a bit before it shows up again. Give it a little more time."

"Me, I'd be happy to never see it again," Harris said. "It's not natural, a ghost gallivanting around as real as you please. Ghosts should stay in the ghost world and leave us breathing folks alone."

"The ghost world?"

"People must have some kind of place to go to when they die. I know all about heaven and hell but it seems to me ghosts wouldn't come from there on account of heaven has a gate and hell has that dog."

Fargo was finding it harder to keep his poker face. "Who told you heaven has a gate?"

"Some parson. He said that when we die, we go up in the clouds and there's this gent called Peter who stands at a gate and lets us in if we've been good or else sends us down to the dog if we've been bad."

"I think you got it mixed up," Clymer said. "I don't think that dog is in the Bible. It's from one of those nursery poems mothers are always saying to their sprouts."

"I do not have it mixed up. And they're not nursery poems. They're called nursery rhymes."

"Don't get all prickly."

"Then don't call me dumb. Besides, what do you know about rhymes. You told me your ma walked out on your pa when you were two."

"My aunt raised me, after. She read to me some when I was little."

Harris glanced at Fargo. "What do you say? You ever read the Bible? Is there a dog in there or not?"

"Can't say as I've heard there is, no."

"Well, if the dog ain't in there, it's somewhere, and if there is a dog, then it won't let ghosts come floating up here to spook us."

"You have it all figured out."

Harris nodded. "I've thought about where we go after we die, sure. Who doesn't? I think on it most when I'm drunk because when I'm not drunk I don't have a lot of thoughts in my head."

"I wouldn't mind being drunk right now," Fargo said.

Clymer responded with, "Me either. It's hard not being allowed to take a nip now and then. I hate milk. And beer just doesn't taste the same. What else is there?"

"I get by with water when I have to."

"I wonder if ghosts drink," Harris said.

"Use your head," Clymer told him. "Ghosts walk through walls and such. They couldn't drink no more than they could eat."

Fargo had an inspiration. "Has this ghost walked through any trees?"

"How's that?"

"This ghost of yours. Does it walk through the trees or around them?"

Clymer scratched his stubble. "You know, I don't rightly know."

"It just sort of glides around all spooky-looking," Harris said. "Sort of like a butterfly only without the wings."

Fargo scanned the woods but there was nothing. "Maybe it's gone back to the ghost world."

"Could be," Harris agreed. "Ghosts don't stick around very long. I heard of a haunted house once where the ghost only acted up for a few minutes each night but that was enough to scare the people who live there half out of their hides."

"I just thought of something," Clymer said. "If ghosts are real, does this mean those other things are, too? Fairies and whatnot?"

Harris snorted. "You mean those little people with wings that flit about like hummingbirds? They ain't real. Leprechauns, neither. Although I met an Irishman once who swore he'd seen one."

Just when Fargo thought their talk couldn't get any more ridiculous, it did.

"What about those ladies with fish tails that live in the sea? And those hairy critters some Injuns says live deep in the mountains?"

"I ain't never been to the ocean so I can't say about those fish women. Although I met me a river rat once who had been on a ship and he told me those fish gals are as real as you and me. They sit on rocks and wriggle their tails to lure sailors into the sea so they can drown them."

"It sure is a strange world," Clymer said.

For Fargo it got a lot stranger as just then a pale— *something*—seemed to float into view off in the woods. He blinked but it was still there. "What the hell?"

"I told you!" Clymer exclaimed. "And you were thinking we were simpletons, I bet."

"Keep your voice down," Harris cautioned. "Ghosts don't like loud noises."

"Says who?" Clymer demanded.

"Why, just about everybody. Yell at a ghost and it ske-daddles. The same as if you throw water that those Catholics wash their feet in."

"Hush," Fargo said. He heard an odd lilting cry.

"The ghost keeps doing that," Harris whispered. "If it was closer I'd chuck a rock at it."

"Let's go see what it is," Fargo said, and started into the trees. He had gone half a dozen steps when he realized neither man was following him. "What are you waiting for?"

"I ain't hankering to talk to no ghost," Harris said. "It might get in my head and make me growl like a dog and spit on people."

"You're thinking of demons," Clymer said.

"Oh. That's right. I get them confused. I never did believe in demons much but now that ghosts are real, demons must be, too."

"I'd sure like to meet one of those fish gals. I wonder if she'd be good to eat? I'm powerful fond of cooked fish."

Fargo made a mental note to look these two up the next time he was sitting around camp bored. Drawing his Colt, he moved deeper into the trees. The pale figure was still moving about. It was definitely on two legs, not four. It was weaving among the trees at a peculiar shuffling gait. He slowed and crept quietly forward. Suddenly a twig crunched under his boot.

The thing turned in his direction.

Fargo's skin crawled. It was coming toward him. He raised the Colt but he didn't shoot. Not yet. Not until he knew what it was and if it was a threat. The lilting cry began again, only it wasn't a cry at all.

The thing was singing.

Fargo lowered the Colt as the figure shuffled to within a dozen steps. That close, he could see it was a woman. An old woman with a wild mane of hair as gray as smoke, wearing a doeskin dress so worn and faded it was ready to fall apart.

She was singing in Lakota in a voice that cracked and rasped as if there was something wrong with her throat.

"I will not harm you," Fargo said in her tongue.

The woman came closer, moving with that odd shuffling way she had.

It wasn't until he could practically reach out and touch her that Fargo realized why. Her left foot, and probably her whole left leg judging by how her dress clung to it, was withered and deformed. So was her left arm and hand. She stopped and he saw her face clearly, and understood.

Someone, somewhere, had struck the woman a brutal blow. The left half of her forehead had caved in, and the left half of her face resembled a withered fig. Her left eye was white and sightless.

Fargo suspected a tomahawk or war club was to blame, that perhaps the woman's village had been raided and she had done as any Lakota woman would do and defended her loved ones and her band, and been struck.

The woman stopped singing and crooked a gnarled finger at him. "Have you seen her, white-eye?"

"Seen who?"

"My girl. I cannot find her. She was with me when they attacked but now she is gone."

"How are you known?"

The woman tilted her head. "I am half a woman. Once I was a whole woman but those days are gone."

Fargo looked into her good eye. It held a gleam that wasn't normal, a bright, sparkling glint that hinted at madness, or a mental state close to it.

"I gave up my name when I lost my daughter. What good was it? A name is a flower that does not last the winter. A name dies when we die." She tittered in that raspy voice of hers. "I have no need of a name now. I am not here and will not be here until I find her."

"Where is your man?"

The right half of her face became etched in sorrow. "I lost him when I lost my little girl. They killed him. A lance through the chest. I tried to pull it out but I was not strong enough." She pressed her good hand to her withered hand and rubbed them. "So much blood. Blood on my hands, blood on my arms, blood on my face, blood on my dress."

"Try not to think of it," Fargo said softly.

She tittered, then touched the withered side of her face. "That is when I got this. I took my husband's knife and tried to stab one of them and he hit me. They thought I was dead but I came back to life, and now I look for my girl. My sweet, precious girl."

Fargo had been right. Her village had been raided, her husband slain, her child taken or killed, and she had her skull bashed in. "Where are your people?" He worried that her village was near. Someone might come looking for her and spot the senator's camp.

"They are where they are. I am where I am. I do not care about them."

"Why not?"

"They say my head is in a whirl. They say my baby is dead when I know my baby is alive. I look for her everywhere."

"How long ago was your village attacked?"

"How long?" The woman scrunched up the good half of her face. "Was it yesterday? Or twenty sleeps ago?" She tittered some more. "I would count them on my fingers but only half my fingers work."

Fargo had a thought. "How many winters have you lived?"

"Twenty-seven. Or maybe it is twenty-six. I forget things like that. I forget many things but I never forget my baby." She turned to the right and the left. "Where can she be? I miss her so much. My heart is heavy."

Fargo couldn't get over how old the woman looked. He'd taken her to be sixty or more. "You should not wander around at night. There are bears and mountain lions."

"Her name is Morning Dew. Do you like her name? I think it is the prettiest name there ever could be."

"It is a fine name." Fargo motioned toward camp. "Why not come and sit by our fire? We have food and water."

"I do not want to eat. I do not want to drink. I only want my girl." The woman started to walk away.

Boots thudded, and Harris and Clymer came up on either side of Fargo. Their rifles were leveled but they merely gaped.

"Well, I'll be," Harris declared. "She ain't no ghost. I figured she couldn't be when we saw you talking to her because ghosts don't talk much unless they're making spooky sounds."

"It's an old Sioux," Clymer said. "Where's she going? What's she doing out here, anyhow? Doesn't she know better than to walk around in the wild at night? That's what the day is for."

The woman turned.

"Look at her face!" Harris exclaimed.

"She's scarier than any ghost."

The woman fixed her good eye on Fargo. "Are these your brothers?"

"They are Heyokas."

"They are clowns? Do they do everything backward?"

"They try their best."

The woman gave half a smile and a little wave and shuffled into the darkness, singing.

With a start, Fargo recognized the song. It was one Lakota mothers often sang to small children when they tucked them in at night.

"She's downright peculiar," was Clymer's opinion.

"Shouldn't we stop her?" Harris asked. "She'll tell her tribe where to find us and we'll be up to our neck in redskins."

"Let her go," Fargo said.

"I don't mind shooting her. I've never shot a female but I'm not hankering to be scalped."

"No."

"Whatever you say. I just hope you're not making a mistake."

So did Fargo.

12

Senator Fulton Keever was in fine fettle the next morning. He came out of his tent all smiles and saying good morning to everyone. In his wake trailed Gerty, who scowled at the world and everyone in it. Rebecca emerged last and was her usual quiet self. She glanced at Fargo only once, and when she did there were daggers in her eyes.

Fargo hunkered by the fire, sipping coffee. He hadn't slept well. Add to that his frame of mind over the shenanigans going on, and he was in a testy mood.

Senator Keever came over and clapped him on the back. "How are you, sir, this morning? Have you made up your mind? Are you leaving us and heading back to civilization?"

"No."

"I won't hold it against you if you do. But I wish you would reconsider. I hired you for a specific reason. You are supposed to be the best there is at what you do, and I—" Keever stopped. "Wait? What did you say?"

"I'm not going anywhere."

Whether by coincidence or intent, just then Owen and his human shadow, Lichen, strolled over.

"Did you hear him, Mr. Owen?" the senator said. "Apparently he has decided to stay with us, after all."

"I heard." Owen grinned as if he found it funny. "You're glad, I bet, all the trouble you've gone to."

Keever coughed. "Yes, yes, of course. I was a little surprised, is all. He seemed so determined to leave us last night."

Gerty said, "I wish he would. I don't like people who don't treat me nice. I don't like them at all."

"I know," Keever said. "I've heard you say that a million times. But be a dear and don't interrupt when the adults are talking, all right?"

"I'll talk when I want. I'll say what I want. If I don't like someone, I'll say that, too."

Owen was staring at Fargo. "What's this I hear about some squaw paying us a visit last night?"

"What's that?" Senator Keever said.

Fargo nodded. "She was harmless. Touched in the head. But it worries me, her showing up like that. Her village can't be far. I'm going to look around. I want everyone to stay in camp until I get back."

"But I have hunting to do," the senator complained. "I was hoping we could look for sign today."

"When I get back," Fargo stressed.

"Surely if a village was close by, we would know it by now?"

"Not if it's behind one of these hills," Fargo said to set him straight.

"Damn," Owen said. "Just what we needed. I'll keep extra men posted and have the horses ready to light a shuck."

"This complicates things," Keever said.

Fargo finished his coffee and put his tin cup in his saddlebags. He saddled up and was just done adjusting the cinch when Rebecca materialized at his elbow.

"I'm sorry about last night."

"You don't need to apologize for not wanting to die. It shows good sense, and there's a shortage of that around here." Fargo smiled to show there were no hard feelings. So what if she tried to use him? He got to make love to her—and wouldn't mind doing so again.

"Be careful out there. The men are on edge. They're saying we could be attacked anytime."

"I've been trying to get that through your thick heads for days now." Fargo forked leather, the saddle creaking under his weight.

"Remember. Don't trust my husband. I meant what I said about him not being honest with you. I'd say more but if he found out I told you, he would beat me."

Fargo wondered if she was telling the truth or if this was another of her ploys. "I'm not the lunkhead everyone seems to think I am. I suspect the senator is after gold. Is that it?"

Instead of answering, Rebecca asked a question of her own. "Do you think it's true? The rumors, I mean? Is there really gold in these hills?"

"It wouldn't surprise me. But only a fool goes looking for trouble." Fargo gigged the Ovaro. It took a few minutes to find the spot where he had talked to the Lakota woman. The ground was hard and she hadn't left many prints. He tracked her for half an hour until he lost every trace on a rocky spur. By then the sun was well up and the Black Hills were alive with wildlife. That wasn't all. From atop the spur he spied smoke plumes in the distance. It could be her village.

Fargo had to find out. Avoiding the high lines, he cautiously wound through the woods. He spooked a doe that bounded off through the brush making a god-awful amount of racket. It gave him a few anxious moments until he was sure no one was coming to investigate.

The acrid scent of smoke warned him the village was near. Dismounting, Fargo tied the reins to a limb, slid the Henry from the saddle scabbard, and cat-footed to a low knoll. Flattening, he snaked to the top.

Tepees covered scores of acres. A Lakota village, the lodges arranged in circles with the flaps facing one another. Many of the buffalo-hide coverings bore painted symbols. Warriors, women, and children moved unconcernedly about, secure in the knowledge that they were in the heart of their own territory and few enemies would dare attack. Sentries

91

were posted, though, and the horse herd was kept under close guard.

Fargo watched a while. He had lived in a village just like this once. The Sioux were friendlier to whites than they were now. It was before they learned that the white idea of a good Indian was a dead Indian and that those the whites didn't kill were forced onto reservations. Fargo would hate to see that happen to the Sioux. They were a fierce, proud people.

Fargo was about to slide down the knoll and get out of there when he was startled to see two white men on horseback approaching the village openly with no weapons in their hands. He was surprised even more when none of the Sioux showed alarm. Warriors didn't come rushing to confront the intruders. Instead, the pair rode on in as if they belonged there.

It was as they were climbing down that Fargo got his biggest surprise yet. He blinked and looked again, but there was no doubt: the pair were Owen and Lichen.

A Lakota wearing a heavy buffalo robe came out of a lodge and greeted them. After a bit they all went in. The flap closed behind them.

Fargo didn't know what to make of it. Lem Owen had no great love for Indians. For Owen to be down there, he must have a damn good reason.

Time passed. Twice small parties of Sioux passed close to where Fargo lay. When the flap parted and Owen and Lichen emerged, he hurried to the Ovaro. Constantly on the alert for Lakotas, he made for two hills southeast of the village. Anyone leaving had to pass between them.

Fargo stayed well back in the trees until hooves clopped. Owen and Lichen were talking and taking their sweet time. He brought the Ovaro out in front of them and reined broadside. "Look what we have here. Two blood brothers to the Sioux, and they never told anyone."

Owen and Lichen reined up. Lichen didn't appear too happy. Owen chuckled and grinned.

"What the hell are you doing here, Fargo?"

"I could ask you the same thing. You're supposed to be back in camp with the senator."

Lichen snapped, "He's the reason we're here, you jackass. So if you think you can—"

Owen reached over and put a hand on Lichen's arm. "Let me do the talking."

"But—"

"You heard me." Owen casually leaned on his saddle horn. "Don't this beat all. You must have seen us pay that redskin a visit."

"That redskin have a name?"

"Little Face."

Fargo thought he had recognized the medicine man. Little Face always wore a buffalo robe, even in the hottest weather. "I've met the gent. He hates whites as much as he hates anything."

"So how is it he met with us? Is that what you're wondering? I set it up months ago. For the senator."

To say Fargo was confused was putting it mildly. "Start explaining, and make it good. Something tells me I've been lied to, and there better be a reason."

Lichen swore. "Listen to him. Acting as if he's the cock of the walk. Say the word and I'll put a window in his skull."

"I wish you'd try," Fargo said.

Owen cuffed Lichen on the shoulder. "Didn't I just tell you I'd do the talking?"

"Sorry. It's just that he puts on airs."

Owen turned to Fargo and spread his hands. "You have to forgive him, hoss. He has a puny thinker."

"He's not the only one."

Owen ignored the barb and said, "I'll gladly tell you

whatever you want to know. If the senator gets mad, it's his own fault for not telling you himself."

Fargo was immediately suspicious. Owen was being too accommodating. "I'm listening."

"This hunt we're on isn't the real reason the senator came to the Black Hills. He's here on a mission for the government."

Lichen glanced sharply at Owen.

"You see, the government wants to set up peace talks with the Sioux. I don't need to tell you how many whites the Sioux have killed. With more pilgrims flocking west every year, that tally is liable to climb a lot higher unless the government does something."

Fargo didn't say anything.

"They think the answer is a peace treaty. They sent me out last winter to see if the Sioux were willing to meet with Senator Keever. He's on the Council for Indian Affairs, or whatever they call it. Little Face agreed, and here we are." Owen smiled that too-friendly smile of his.

"Why wasn't I told about this when Keever hired me?"

"This whole business is supposed to stay secret. Don't ask me why the government doesn't want word to get out, but they don't." Owen leaned on his saddle horn again. "Keever hired you so the hunt would appear to be legitimate. You've guided other hunters. No one would suspect he was up to something else."

Fargo had to admit it was just like the government to do things behind everyone's back. "Does his wife know?"

"I couldn't say. Rebecca doesn't like my company much."

Fargo noticed that he called her by her first name. "So this is why he refused to leave when I wanted?"

Owen beamed. "You've seen the light." He kneed his horse closer to the Ovaro. "Listen. Keeping you in the dark wasn't my idea."

"Since when did we become pards?"

"We may not always see eye to eye but I know you're a man of your word. I told Keever that if he let you in on it, you wouldn't tell anyone. But he said that it wasn't up to him, that his orders came from higher up and it had to be a secret from practically everybody."

Fargo grew warm with anger. After all the scouting and special work he had done for the army, to find out the government didn't trust him was a kick in the gut. "Son of a bitch."

"Take it up with the senator. He'll be mad at me for telling you but what can he do?"

"I'll take it up with him, all right."

Owen raised his reins. "Now if you'll excuse us, we have to go tell him that Little Face will meet with him tonight at sunset." He paused. "You going back too?"

"No." Fargo had thinking to do, and there was something else.

"Suit yourself. I won't tell Keever you saw us. You can do that yourself." Owen nodded and rode past, Lichen right behind him.

Fargo waited until they were out of sight then shifted in the saddle and stared at a thicket. In the Lakota tongue he said, "You can come out. I saw you sneak up on us."

The young woman in the beaded buckskin dress who had been following Owen and Lichen stepped into the open. "I thought I was careful. You have eyes like an eagle."

"This day is chock-full of surprises," Fargo said in English, and switched to Lakota. "We meet again, Sweet Flower."

"That is not my real name. That is what you call me."

"What is your real name?"

"Sweet Flower will do." She brazenly came over and stood smiling up at him. "I am not unhappy to see you again."

"Oh?" All of a sudden Fargo was in no hurry to get back. He slid his right boot from the stirrup and crooked his leg over the saddle. "You are as beautiful as ever."

"And you are as bold." Sweet Flower laughed. "I should not say this but I have thought of you much since we met."

"I have thought of you too," Fargo fibbed. The turn of events held unexpected promise. "I have thought of your body without that dress on. You would be twice as beautiful."

"No man has ever talked to me as you do."

"Is that so?" Fargo slid down. He deliberately brushed his chest against her bosom and put his hands on her hips. "I have a lot more words to describe you."

"I should not listen."

"Go or stay. It is up to you. But if you stay, you know what I will do." Fargo paused. "Which will it be?"

"I will stay."

13

Fargo learned long ago that when a woman made up her mind that she wanted to share herself with a man there was nothing a man could do but give in to the inevitable. Not that he ever refused a pretty face and an enticing body. He was eager to explore her delights, but there were a few things he wanted to know first. "Why were you following those two white men?"

"It is said they are with other whites. That a white woman and a white girl are with them." Sweet Flower gazed in the direction the pair had gone. "I have never seen a white woman. I would very much like to."

Fargo remembered a tale he once heard about how the first white woman to venture west attended a rendezvous during the fur trapping days and was a sensation with the Indians. Curiosity was as common a trait as skin. He asked his other question. "I thought you were an Oglala?"

"I am."

"The village back there is Miniconjou."

"I am visiting my sister. She is the wife of a Miniconjou warrior and I have not seen her in several winters."

Taking the Ovaro's reins in one hand and Sweet Flower's hand in the other, Fargo went deeper into the trees. She didn't resist. She was looking up at him with a strange look on her face.

"What?"

"I am wondering how it will be. I have never been with a white man before."

"You honor me."

"I want to because of your hair."

About to reach for her, Fargo stopped. "What?"

"She touched his jaw, and grinned. "I would like to kiss and rub a face that is not smooth."

"You sure are female."

Sweet Flower looked down at herself. "What else would I be? If I were male I would not have this body."

Fargo kept on walking. They needed a nice secluded spot for their tryst. It wouldn't do to have Lakota warriors stumble on them in the midst of their passion.

"I have a question."

"I have ears."

"Have you laid with many Indian women?"

"One or two," Fargo answered. The total was more like thirty or forty. He lost count long ago.

"Have you been with an Oglala woman before?"

Fargo tried to recollect. He was sure he had but she might take exception so he hedged by saying, "I have heard that Oglala women please their men better than any other."

Sweet Flower smiled. "My mother taught me that a woman must always excite the man. The more excited he is, the more he pleases the woman."

"Your mother was wise. You can excite me all you want."

"It will be strange. You are different from anyone I have ever touched." Sweet Flower ran her hand over his beard. "I hope all your hair does not blunt my desire."

"I have met many women who like it."

"I thought about you last night and I think making love to you will be like making love to a bear. My grandmother told me once that she thought white men must be part bear because they are so hairy."

"We can stop talking about hair now."

"Do you like mine?"

Fargo was no fool. If she were bald he would say what he now said. "You are beautiful."

"Thank you. You are beautiful too."

"Whites say men are handsome."

"Handsome or beautiful, I like men most when their clothes are off. I have sometimes thought that it would be better if we all went without clothes."

Fargo almost asked if she had been kicked in the head by a horse when she was little but he doubted she would appreciate the joke. "There are whites who think like that. They go around bare-assed naked." He used the English words.

"Bare-assed naked?" Sweet Flower slowly repeated it. "I will remember that, and when I meet whites from now on, I will let them know I like to be bare-assed naked. Would that be nice to do?"

"They will think you are the friendliest female alive."

"Good. Thank you for your advice."

By then they were far enough in and hemmed by so many trees and the undergrowth that Fargo felt safe in tying the Ovaro and leading Sweet Flower to a patch of grass. He stopped and faced her. Admiring the twin peaks that poked at her doeskin dress and the swell of her shapely thighs, he remarked, "You really are beautiful."

She ran her fingers through his beard. "And you really are very hairy."

"You hair a man to death, do you know that?"

"And you say strange thing but I like you anyway." Sweet Flower rose on the tips of her toes and lightly kissed him on the lips. "Kissing you is no different from kissing a man without hair."

"One more word about hair . . ."

"Which word do you want? I have many words."

"I want your body instead." Fargo pulled her close and fused his mouth to hers. For all her talk about wanting him,

99

she was tense and unsure of herself. Gradually, though, she relaxed. When he ran his hands down her back and cupped her bottom, she uttered a tiny moan.

Fargo kissed her ear, the side of her neck, her throat. He slid a hand over her hip to her breast and cupped it. At the contact she trembled slightly, and moaned louder.

Suddenly her hand groped him, low down. Caught by surprise, Fargo stiffened in more ways than one. She cupped him and stroked him and soon had him as hard as iron. Not to be outdone, Fargo pressed his hand against the junction of her thighs. She gave off heat like a stove.

It reached the point where Fargo eased her to the grass and stretched out beside her. He managed to do it without breaking their kiss. Cupping her other breast, he squeezed it through her dress. Her hands rose and removed his hat so she could run her fingers through his hair.

Fargo hiked at her doeskin. It fit so tight that getting it high enough took some doing.

Sweet Flower grew impatient. She pushed him back, sat up, and quickly shed the dress over her head. Carefully placing it next to them, she laid back down and spread her arms.

"I am bare-assed naked," she said proudly.

"You are still wearing moccasins," Fargo teased, and damned if she didn't sit back up and take them off.

"There. Now I am bare-assed naked, yes?"

"As bare-assed as bare-assed can be."

Sweet Flower grinned and plucked at his buckskins. "Now it is your turn. You must be bare-assed naked too."

Fargo envisioned being caught with his britches off by some unfriendly warriors. "How about if I just take off my shirt?"

"It would not be right for you to wear clothes when I am bare-assed naked," Sweet Flower replied. "If you will not be bare-assed naked with me, I will put my dress back on and go."

Fargo proceeded to strip. He made it a point to put his gun belt within easy reach. As he turned to Sweet Flower, she placed her hands on his chest.

"This is strange."

"What is?"

"You have a lot of hair on your head and a lot of hair on your face but you do not have much on your body."

Fargo sighed. "Hair and bare-assed naked. Next you will want to talk about flying pigs."

"Pigs? I am sorry. I not understand. I have seen pigs. They do not have much hair. All they have is skin. Does that make them bare-assed naked? Or can only people be bare-assed naked? And how can they fly when they do not have wings? I am confused."

"Shoot me now and put me out of my misery."

"Sorry? You are hurting?"

"Only between my ears." Fargo kissed her before she could say anything else. He hoped that was the end of the hair business but when he slid his mouth lower and nuzzled her neck, her hand found his manhood and groped around it as if she were searching for something. Then she giggled.

"You do not have much hair there, either."

"Please tell me we are done with hair."

"What you do have is soft and crinkly like my own."

"God in heaven."

"God? That is the white word for the Great Mystery. I do not think the Great Mystery has hair."

Fargo rose onto an elbow and cupped her chin. "Sweet Flower?" he said softly.

"Yes?"

"Say the word hair one more time and you can make love to yourself."

"You sound upset."

"I am, as the whites would say, pissed, and when a man is pissed, it spoils his mood." Fargo went to kiss her.

"I am sorry I pissed you. I have never made love to a white man and I do not know how white men like to do it."

"Without talking. We like to make love to women who keep their mouths shut the whole time."

"Even when we kiss? What if I want to suck on your tongue?"

"One. Two. Three. Four—"

"Why are you counting?"

"I need the practice. Six. Seven. Eight. Nine. Ten." Fargo stared at her."Well?"

"Well what?"

"Is there anything else perfectly stupid you would like to say?"

"But you just told me to keep quiet so I do not piss you. I wish you would make up your mind how you want me to be. I am confused."

Enough was enough. Fargo spread her legs and eased onto his knees between them. He touched the tip of his pole to her slit. Then, without any other foreplay, he rammed up into her. "Piss this."

Sweet Flower came up off the grass with her back in a bow and her luscious lips parted wide. She grabbed him by the back of his head, pulled his face to hers, and gave him a kiss the likes of which few women ever had. Her hands were everywhere, exploring, kneading, caressing.

Now this was more like it, Fargo thought. He pinched a nipple and nipped her earlobe. He sculpted her other breast. All while he rocked on his knees and slowly thrust his hips.

Sweet Flower moaned. She cooed. She breathed molten air. Her nails dug into his shoulders deep enough to draw drops of blood. Her legs rose and her ankles locked behind him.

Fargo took his time. He was in no rush to get back to camp now that he knew the senator's party wasn't in any danger. It had surprised him that the Lakotas would even think of signing a peace treaty, but stranger things had happened.

A loud moan from Sweet Flower signaled her release. Her eyelids fluttered and she churned her bottom.

Her climax was an earthquake that shook Fargo to his core and set off his own eruption. He rammed into her again and again, pounding her until he had no energy left to do more than sink down on top of her and rest his cheek on her breasts. He closed his eyes.

After a while Sweet Flower asked, "Did I make you happy?"

"You would make any man happy."

Sweet Flower smiled and playfully pulled at his beard. "This tickled me. I almost laughed a few times."

Fargo didn't care to get her started on hair again so he didn't respond.

"If I ask you for a favor, will you do it?"

Half dreading it would be something silly, Fargo said, "That depends on the favor."

"I still want to see the white woman and her child. I heard Little Face and the one called Owen mention them. I would like to see the kind of clothes they wear and how they do their hair."

Fargo was more interested in something else. "They were talking and not using sign language? I did not know Little Face speaks the white tongue."

"The one called Owen speaks Lakota."

This was news to Fargo, too. Owen must have had previous dealings with the Sioux. "Where did you hear them talk?"

"They were in Little Face's lodge. I only heard a little. It is not polite to listen outside lodges."

"How do your people feel about the treaty?"

"The what?"

"A man has come from the Great White Father to talk

peace with the Lakotas. The White Father wants the Sioux to sign a paper that says the Sioux will never again kill another white."

"No one told me this. All I heard them talk about was the—" Sweet Flower stopped, and stiffened.

Fargo looked up. She was staring over his shoulder at something behind him. He twisted to see what she was seeing—and his gut balled into a knot.

Not ten feet away stood several warriors. Two had arrows nocked to their bowstrings, the strings pulled back, the shafts ready to fly.

The third warrior was Little Face, the Lakota who hated him.

14

Fargo went to reach for his Colt.

"Touch it and die, white dog."

Fargo froze. He didn't doubt the threat would be carried out. The two warriors with Little Face looked eager to sink their arrows into him.

Sweet Flower shifted from under him. "What is the meaning of this?"

"I saw you follow the white men who came to our village," Little Face said in his usual flinty tone. He wore his buffalo robe, and his face was pinched in displeasure. A small face, it was, much too small for a man his size, which was why he had the name he did. "I came after you to find out why, daughter."

Fargo was flabbergasted. He glanced from her to Little Face and back again and didn't see any resemblance at all.

"I asked Long Forelock and Bear Loves to come with me and help me stop you," Little Face had gone on. "I have planned for too long to have you ruin things."

"I wanted to see the white woman," Sweet Flower said.

Little Face grunted. "Instead I find you lying with the white man I most want dead." He glared at Fargo. "We meet again, He Who Walks Many Trails. I have waited a long time for this."

Sweet Flower gave a start. "*This* white man is the one you always talk about? The one you want to kill so much?"

"You did not know?"

"I did not see him when he came to our village that time. I was with Left Handed Buffalo then, remember?" Sweet Flower calmly picked up her dress. "I am sorry to lie with your enemy, Father."

"That you would lie with *any* white man saddens me. You know how I feel about them."

"I was curious."

Little Face sighed. "Your mother was the same way. She tested my patience just as you do."

"I miss her," Sweet Flower said.

"I miss her, too. She was a brave woman. She took a Blackfoot arrow meant for me." Little Face stared at Fargo. "I wanted a white woman to take her place but this one persuaded the council to let her go back to her people."

Fargo finally found his voice. "Tell your daughter why you wanted a white wife."

"Why did you, Father?" Sweet Flower asked.

Little Face's smile was positively vicious. "So I could treat her as she deserved. Every day I would beat her. Every day I would kick her and spit on her. Every day she would wish she could die but I would not let her. It would have given me great pleasure."

Something occurred to Fargo. "If you hate whites so much, why did you agree to talk peace with them?"

Little Face squatted, his dark eyes glittering with delight. "Do you truly think I would? Knowing me as you do?"

"No."

"You know me well." Little Face grinned. "I will tell you why I have agreed to meet this Kee-ver. But first." He turned to his daughter. "Go back to our village and wait in our lodge. We will talk when I am done here."

Fargo saw that she had put her dress on. He thought maybe she would say something on his behalf but she didn't even look at him.

"As you wish, Father. Again, I am sorry."

"I am disappointed. But you did not know. Now go. I have much to do."

Sweet Flower put a hand on Little Face's shoulder. "Be careful, Father." With that, she was gone, sprinting off through the trees.

Little Face turned back to Fargo. "Life holds many surprises, does it not? You did not guess that you are here because of me."

"I must have missed something?"

"Heed me. Listen and learn, for you do not have long to live." Little Face was enjoying himself. "I have hated you since you took the white woman from me. I would have killed you that night for asking the council to spare her but you have too many friends among the Lakota. They would be angry with me."

Fargo glanced at Long Forelock and Bear Loves, hoping they would lower their bows so he could try for his Colt.

"I had to swallow my anger. I had to hold my hate inside and let you ride from our village. But I vowed to have my revenge. I spent many long nights thinking how to do it. I needed to lure you back without you knowing it was me who lured you."

"You speak with two tongues. I am not here because of you. I was hired to guide the man the Father of all the whites sent to talk peace with the Lakotas."

"Who do you think got word to this man asking him to come? Who do you think suggested he ask you to be his guide?"

Fargo wasn't buying it. "You still speak with two tongues. How could you know to contact Senator Keever?" He had to use the English words since there were no Lakota words for "senator" or "Keever." "How would you get word to him?" Even as he asked, the answer hit him with the force of a physical blow.

"The one called Owen went to this Kee-ver for me. It was

Owen who told Kee-ver that you should be his guide. Owen did so because I asked him to. I led him to think you were my friend."

The sheer deviousness of Little Face's scheme began to sink in. "You son of a bitch," Fargo said in English.

Little Face laughed. "You are mad. Good. You will be even madder when I tell you the rest." He folded his arms across his knees. "My inviting this Kee-ver to talk peace came to me in a vision."

Fargo kept glancing at the other two. But, damn them, they held their bows steady.

"I have counted coup on whites," Little Face rambled on. "Many Lakotas have. Yet no matter how many we kill, more keep coming to our land. They do not fear us as they should, as our other enemies do, and I want the whites to fear us. I want them to fear us so much, they will never set foot in Sioux country again."

"Nothing you can do would make them fear you that much. They will think nothing of it."

"In my vision I saw differently. In my vision I saw a pack of wolves trying to bring down a bull elk. The elk gored them with its antlers and kicked them with its hooves. But no matter how many it hurt or killed, the wolves did not give up. They kept coming, again and again."

Fargo waited. There would be a point to this. There was always a point to a vision.

"Then the leader of the pack leaped at the elk's throat and the elk caught the wolf on its antlers and pinned it to the ground and an antler pierced its heart and it died. Do you know what happened next?"

Fargo refused to answer.

"The rest of the wolves went away. Their leader was dead and they gave up the fight. Do you understand? Do you see what that meant?"

"I am sure you will tell me."

"The bull elk was my people. The wolves were white men. For the white men to go away and not bother my people, we must kill one of their leaders. We must kill a man high in their councils, a man they all know, so that when they hear he is dead, it will fill them with fear and they will stay away from our land." Little Face smiled smugly.

The devil of it was, Fargo reflected, that killing a United States senator *would* create quite a stir. Every newspaper in the country would carry the story. People would be more fearful than ever of venturing into Sioux territory. "Why did you pick Keever?"

"I asked Owen to tell me who was great in white councils. He could only think of a few, which surprised me." Little Face uttered a snort of disgust. "I have always known whites are stupid, but to not know their own leaders. When I asked Owen how this could be, he told me that he had no interest in what whites call . . ." He stopped, his brow furrowed as he tried to recall the word.

"Politics," Fargo guessed.

"Yes. That is it. Owen said the Great White Father would not come himself but he might send what he called a sen-a-tor, who is almost as high in white councils." Little Face's eyes narrowed. "He spoke straight tongue? This sen-a-tor is an important white?"

Fargo thought fast. "No. A senator is not high in white councils. Kill him and the other whites will not notice."

Little Face grinned. "You talk with two tongues."

"Think what you want," Fargo said with a shrug.

"I think that when I meet with this Sen-a-tor Kee-ver at sunset, I will invite him into my lodge and give him drink and food. I will make him think I am a friend, and when I am ready, when he least expects, I will cut his throat from ear to ear. Or maybe I will bind him and cut off parts of his body to test his courage."

"What about Owen?"

"Will I let him live, you mean?" Little Face's grin widened. "Someone must go back and tell the whites what happened."

Fargo had to hand it to the wily devil. As plans went, it wasn't half bad. "You have this well thought out."

"There is more. After I kill this Kee-ver, I will take his woman as my own. I will do to her all the things I wanted to do to that other white woman, the one you saved. I will beat her. I will have her eat what a dog would eat. I will make her weep and grovel at my feet, and this time you cannot stop me."

"I will not need to. Your plan has flaws."

"A vision is always true. You know that. You have lived with us."

Yes, Fargo had, and yes, he knew how much stock they placed in their visions. The Lakotas would go off alone and do without food and water for days in the hope a vision would come to them. "What about after what you saw in your vision?"

Little Face appeared puzzled. "After?"

"Yes. After you kill Keever and take his woman. Have you thought that far ahead? Killing him will cause some whites fear but it will make many more mad. The Great White Father will be mad, and he will send his blue coats against the Lakotas in numbers as great as the blades of grass on the prairie."

Little Face laughed.

"The whites will do to the Lakotas as they have done to many other tribes," Fargo went on. "Their soldiers will build forts where they will be safe from your arrows and lances. When they come out, your people will kill some of them and they will kill some of you. But always when you kill them, more soldiers will come to take their place. Bit by bit they will whittle you down to where there will be so many of them and so few of you that there will come a day when they drive you from your land." Fargo paused. His talking served a purpose. He was hoping to lull the other two into finally lowering their bows.

"I do not believe you."

"Thousands of Lakotas will die and it will be your fault. Your hate will bring sadness to their hearts and an end to their ways." Fargo could have yipped with glee when Long Forelock let his bow dip so that the arrow was pointing at the ground. Bear Loves, though, hadn't lowered his.

"You try to put fear in my heart. Fear for my people. But I do this for them. To keep them safe, and our land safe."

Fargo wondered. Little Face had always flattered himself that he was a man of great importance. "Is that all there is to it? Or is it so that you want to stand higher in their eyes?"

"I will enjoy killing you more than I have enjoyed killing any enemy ever," Little Face declared.

"I am not an enemy of the Lakotas," Fargo tried.

"You are *my* enemy. You are my enemy because you are white. You are my enemy because you stopped me from taking that white woman. And now you are my enemy because you have been with my daughter." Little Face's features hardened. "I will stake you out and skin you. I will chop off your fingers and toes. I will dig out your eyes. When I tire of your screams, I will cut out your tongue. It will bring me much happiness."

Fargo almost gave a start. Bear Loves had started to lower his bow. Not much, only a few inches.

"The whites have a word for man like you," Fargo said. "I think you know what it means." He bent toward Little Face and smiled to add salt to the verbal wound. "That word is bastard."

Little Face lost his temper. Snarling, he whipped a knife from under his buffalo robe, and lunged. In doing so, he threw himself between Fargo and Bear Loves, which was exactly what Fargo wanted. Grabbing Little Face's wrists,

Fargo heaved upward. He was buck naked but that hardly mattered when any moment he might be dead. He saw Bear Loves step to the right for a clear shot and he instantly stepped to the left, keeping Little Face between them.

"Subdue him!" Little Face yelled at the others.

Long Forelock flung down his bow, streaked out a knife, and started to come around him.

Fargo's intent was to reach the Ovaro. The Henry was still in the saddle scabbard. Once he got his hands on it, they would answer for their arrogance. Or if need be, he could escape and come back later. He had spare buckskins in his saddlebags, an older set that needed mending, but they would do.

"Help me!" Little Face fumed.

Bear Loves was gliding to the left.

Fargo risked all on a desperate gamble. He swung Little Face at Bear Loves, and shoved. Little Face squawked and tripped and they both went down, tangled together. Long Forelock thrust with his knife but Fargo was ready. He side-stepped and landed a solid cross to the jaw that jolted Long Forelock back.

The way to the Ovaro was clear.

Fargo took a bound, only to have Bear Loves fling out a leg and hook his ankle. Fargo tried to stay on his feet but gravity took over and he landed hard on his hands and chest. He pushed up and was almost to his knees when the razor tip of a knife was jabbed against his neck.

"Are you ready to die?"

15

Through a haze of pain Skye Fargo heard a chuckle. He opened his eyes and glared at his tormentor. "You son of a bitch," he rasped in English.

Little Face laughed. He wagged the knife he was holding, then jabbed Fargo hard in the side. Not deep, but it drew more blood. "I know those words. A blue coat I killed once used them many times while I was cutting on him."

Switching to Lakota, Fargo said, "You have no honor."

"You are my enemy. A warrior counts coup on his enemies. Whether the warrior does it slow or quickly is up to him. With you it will be slow."

Fargo was suspended between two trees. Rope dug into each wrist. His skin was rubbed raw and dry blood caked his forearms. It felt like his whole body was a mass of bruises and welts. Little Face had beat on him with a tree limb for a good quarter of an hour. He was cut in a dozen places. But none of the blows or the cuts were intended to kill him.

"You will suffer greatly before I am done," Little Face boasted. "You will weep and gnash your teeth and beg me to end your misery."

"Don't hold your breath, bastard."

"Eh?" Little Face jabbed him again. "In the Lakota tongue, remember? Or should I cut yours out so you can not talk at all?"

"It will be hard to beg without my tongue."

Little Face's smile was vicious. "You can whimper." He turned away.

Fargo fought down a wave of fury. It would be pointless to lose his temper. There was nothing he could do. He was helpless, completely at the mercy of a bitter enemy.

A rattle drew Fargo's gaze to Long Forelock and Bear Loves. The pair had made a pile of his clothes and upended his saddlebags and were gambling for his effects with a pair of plum-stone dice. So far, Bear Loves had won the Arkansas toothpick and his shirt. Long Forelock had won the Colt and his pants. Neither had won the Henry yet.

Little Face wasn't taking part; he was interested in only one thing.

Fargo tried to swallow but his mouth was too dry. Beads of sweat dribbled down his brow. One got into his eye and stung like hell.

Little Face conversed with the other two in low tones, then came back. "They have agreed to watch you while I am gone."

"You are going somewhere?"

"Have you forgotten?" Little Face pointed to the west with his blood-tipped knife.

The sun was an hour from setting.

"I must prepare for the sen-a-tor."

Fargo *had* almost forgotten. And there he hung, powerless to do anything. "It will be your fault when the soldiers come and wipe out your people."

"The blue coats are no match for the Lakotas. Their horses are slow. They do not shoot straight. Many are boys. They huddle around their campfires at night, in fear we will take their hair." Little Face sneered. "*Them* wipe us out?"

Fargo grasped at a straw. "Senator Keever wanted me at the meeting to translate for him."

"The one called Owen knows enough of our tongue. If the sen-a-tor asks, I will tell him I have not seen you, and say how sad I am that you are not there since you and I are good friends." Little Face sneered in sadistic delight and raised the knife.

Fargo braced for another cut but all his tormentor did was prick his arm, and chortle.

"I leave you now. My friends will watch over you. I have told them that if you try to slip free they are to cut out one of your eyes." Little Face pricked him again. "If you yell they are to sew your mouth shut." He smacked Fargo on the jaw, wheeled, and hiked off.

Fargo sagged. It would be easy to give in to despair. But it wasn't his way. He had never given up his whole life and he would be damned if he would start now.

Long Forelock and Bear Loves were so engrossed in their gambling, they were paying him no mind.

Gritting his teeth, Fargo twisted his wrists. The pain was awful. But if he could get his wrists to bleed again, it would make the rope slick enough for him to work a hand loose. The threat of losing an eye was nothing compared to the threat of losing his life.

The shadows in the woods lengthened. The breeze picked up. Somewhere a robin was warbling.

Fargo kept on twisting. He didn't want to die like this. He'd always figured his end would be quick, a bullet to the brain or an arrow to the heart. Or better yet, to die in bed with a woman, to keel over while making love. Rough for the woman, but the man would go out with a smile on his face. The thought made him chuckle.

Long Forelock glanced at him and said something to Bear Loves, who got up and came over.

Fargo stood perfectly still.

Bear Loves was suspicious. He looked at the ropes and then looked Fargo up and down. "Why did you laugh?"

"I am happy."

"Your head must be in a whirl. You have nothing to be

happy about, stupid one. By the rising of the sun tomorrow you will be dead."

Fargo grasped at another straw. "Has Little Face told you about the white man called Keever? About what he plans to do?"

Bear Loves grunted.

"You do not care that it will cause war to break out? Not war as you are used to it. Not war where you raid an enemy's village and the enemy raids yours. In this war, the blue coats will come again and again. They will kill and kill until the Lakotas are no more."

"You try to make me fear for my people so I will free you. But Little Face warned us you would try that." Bear Loves poked Fargo in the chest. "Do not make noise and do not bother us. The next time, I will cut off one of your fingers or maybe a toe."

As soon as the pair resumed their dice game, Fargo set to work on his wrists. Trickles of blood held promise.

Time crawled, dragged by anchors of worry. Fargo stopped twisting whenever one of the warriors looked in his direction, which wasn't often. Like many Indians—and whites—the Sioux were inveterate gamblers. They would bet on anything—dice, horse races, contests of skill, you name it.

The sun sank. Fargo figured the pair would light a fire but they went on rolling by the light of the moon, bending close over the dice after each toss. He wondered why, and then it hit him. They didn't want a fire for the same reason Little Face hadn't taken him back to the village. A fire might bring other warriors to investigate, and some might be friends of his.

Fargo rested. The way things were going, he'd rub clear down to the bone before he got loose. The pain was awful. Despair nipped at him but he fought it off.

Then a hand touched his shoulder from behind.

Fargo nearly gave a start. He felt fingers slide down his

back, and a warm body pressed against his. Breath fanned his ear and a familiar voice whispered, "I will cut the ropes. Do not let on."

It was the last person Fargo expected. He held his arms still in case the warriors glanced his way. In moments it was done, and lips brushed his other ear.

"We will sneak away. I will go first and you follow."

"No," Fargo whispered. He wasn't leaving without his clothes and his weapons.

"They will kill you."

"They will try." Fargo glanced over his shoulder. "Give me your knife."

Sweet Flower took a step back. "I cannot," she whispered. "They are my people." And with that, she turned and melted into the undergrowth.

Fargo supposed he couldn't blame her. She had gone against her own father in freeing him. Little Face would be furious if he found out, and punish her severely.

Fargo turned toward Long Forelock and Bear Loves. They were rolling dice for the Henry. Both were tense with eagerness. Few Lakotas owned Henrys. It was a trophy any of them would give anything to possess. They were so intent on the dice that neither noticed when Fargo edged toward them. His gun belt lay to one side, where Long Forelock had placed it after winning it.

Bear Loves was about to roll. He stared at the Henry as if by doing so he could will the rifle into his possession. Then his hand flicked and the dice tumbled onto the ground.

Both warriors bent lower then ever, nearly bumping heads.

Fargo sprang. His bare feet made little sound, and he had the gun belt in his left hand and was drawing the Colt with his right before either of them realized he was free. They whirled, Bear Loves grabbing the toothpick and Long Forelock swooping a hand to a knife at his hip.

"I will kill you if you try," Fargo warned. He had no hankering to put windows in their skulls. They hadn't harmed him. The only thing they had done was bind him.

The pair froze, but only for a few seconds. Then Long Forelock glanced at Bear Loves, and nodded, and simultaneously, Long Forelock's other hand swept up off the ground holding a handful of dirt.

Fargo ducked but some of the dirt got into his eyes. He backpedaled and blinked to clear them, and as he did iron fingers clamped onto his wrist and a foot hooked behind his ankle and tripped him.

Long Forelock raised his knife high to stab.

Flat on his back, Fargo pointed the Colt at the warrior's chest, and fired. The blast would carry for a mile. With it came a flash and the smell of the powder.

Long Forelock staggered. He looked down at himself in disbelief and tried to say something but all that came out was blood. Half turning, he reached out for Bear Loves, who was rigid with shock. His fingers clawed in appeal, he mewed like a kitten, and died.

If Fargo had thought to spare Bear Loves, he had another think coming. The death of his friend filled the other warrior with blind rage. Uttering a sharp cry, he threw himself forward.

The toothpick against the Colt was no contest. Fargo rolled, heaved onto a knee, and thumbed back the hammer. But as he went to squeeze the trigger, Bear Loves lashed out with a foot. It caught Fargo on his wrist. Sheer agony shot up his arm, and the Colt fell from fingers gone briefly numb.

Fargo lunged to snatch it up but Bear Loves was quicker. The toothpick arced at his neck. He barely got a hand up in time to grab Bear Loves' wrist; the tip of the blade came within an inch of his jugular.

Bear Loves drove a knee at Fargo's face but Fargo

avoided it and drove his fist into the warrior's gut, doubling him over. It put Bear Loves' chin within easy reach of an uppercut that lifted him onto his toes.

Bear Loves tottered. His ankle caught on Fargo's saddle-bags. He tried to right himself, and in flailing his arms, partly turned. He crashed down on his side and didn't move.

Fargo quickly reclaimed the Colt. He nudged Bear Loves with his toe but the warrior just lay there. Since Fargo hadn't hit him hard enough to knock him out, he suspected the Lakota was playing possum. "Sit up. I will not shoot you unless you force me."

Bear Loves was as still as a log.

Warily, Fargo rolled him over. The warrior's eyes were open, and empty of life. The hilt of the toothpick, jutting between Bear Loves' ribs, explained why; he had fallen on the blade.

"I'll be damned." Fargo yanked it out and wiped it clean on Bear Loves' leggings.

The crunch of a twig brought him around in a blur. But he didn't shoot. "You came back?"

"I never left." Sweet Flower sadly regarded the fallen warriors. "They were friends of mine."

"I did not want to kill them."

"I know. I saw." She put a hand to her forehead. "I wish there had been another way."

"This is on your father's shoulders, not mine or yours," Fargo assured her. He began gathering up his clothes. "What is your real name?"

"Sorry?" she asked absently, still gazing at the dead men.

"Sweet Flower is the name I gave you. What is your real name. You never told me."

"I am called Lame Deer but I like Sweet Flower better."

Fargo tugged into his pants. "Then that is what I will call you." He scooped up his shirt. "Why did you cut me free?"

"It was a hard decision. I do not agree with what my father wants to do. I think that killing the white chief is bad medicine, and many of my people may die."

"They will," Fargo confirmed.

"Your chief, this Kee-ver, came to our lodge as the sun was setting. My father sent me away so I came to get you. You must save this Kee-ver. Tell him of my father's trick, and see that he leaves our land."

"Keever is still alive?" Fargo thought Little Face would have killed him by now.

"I do not know when Father plans to do it. I heard him invite Kee-ver to a feast tomorrow night in his honor, so maybe that is when."

"But it could still be tonight," Fargo mused out loud.

"Yes."

Fargo began strapping on his gun belt. He winced each time he turned a wrist. "Thank you for helping me. It took great courage."

"I am not my father. I do not hate whites because they are different. I do not think all whites are bad. You are white, and you are a good man."

Fargo could think of a parson or three who would disagree. His fondness for women, booze, and cards qualified him as a sinner of the highest order, as a man of the cloth once told him. Not that he had any intention of changing his ways. He might be able to give up whiskey and poker, but women? He wasn't born in a monastery.

"What will you do now?" Sweet Flower asked.

"Go to your village and get Senator Keever out." Fargo couldn't take the chance that Little Face would wait.

"Try that, and you will surely die."

16

Fargo sat so he could pull his boots on.

"Did you hear me? You will never get near my father's lodge. Not with all the people."

Fargo had lived in a Sioux village. Except when special ceremonies were held, after dark it was usually quiet. Families ate, friends visited the lodges of friends, lovers went for walks under a blanket. It should be simple for him to slip in, and he said so.

"You forget. The bands have gathered to see the white buffalo. In our village are Miniconjou, Oglalas, Brules, Hunkpapas, Sans Arcs. There is much moving about and talking and singing."

"I have to try." Fargo had a thought. "How many know of your father's plan to kill the senator?"

"They did," Sweet Flower said with a nod at the bodies. "Perhaps two or three others. Most believe he is meeting with the white chief to make peace with the whites. A lot do not like it but they trust my father to do what is right."

Fargo finished putting himself together. He adjusted his gun belt and then his bandanna, and pulled his hat brim low. "How close can we get on horseback?"

"As far as an arrow can fly twice. But if you are caught—"

"I will say I am with the senator." Fargo forked leather, gritting his teeth against the pain. His wrists hurt like hell and his body was sore all over. He offered her his arm. "Swing up."

Another moment, and they were under way, Sweet Flower with her arms around his waist.

"You do not listen very well. If you are killed, the one called Kee-ver dies, and there will be war with the whites."

Fargo had to try. He picked his way through the forest with care, Sweet Flower pointing the way. They stopped whenever they heard sounds but twice it was only deer and once, at a distance, riders who faded into the night.

The village, as Fargo suspected, turned out to be the same village he saw before. He left the Ovaro in the trees and snaked to the top of the rise, Sweet Flower at his side.

Just as she had said, far more Lakotas than usual were moving about the circles. It was rare for all the bands to get together, and they were having a grand time.

"Which lodge belongs to your father?"

Sweet Flower pointed.

Fargo sighed. It figured. The lodge was clear across a circle. To reach it, he must get past dozens of Sioux.

"I warned you."

"Stay here." Fargo hurried to the Ovaro. Taking off his hat, he placed it on the saddle horn. Then he untied his bedroll, draped a blanket over his head and shoulders, and jogged back to the rise.

Sweet Flower regarded him with a mix of amusement and disbelief. "It will not fool them."

"Why not?" Fargo wanted to know. It was common for warriors to go about with a blanket over them, and for young lovers to stand under blankets to have privacy.

"Your beard. They will take one look at you and know you are not Lakota."

"Not if I keep my head down."

"You are too tall. And you wear boots, not moccasins."

"I will slouch, and I will go barefoot." So saying, Fargo removed his spurs and his boots and laid them on the rise.

Sweet Flower had a litany of objections. "Your feet are

too white, and you do not walk like an Indian. You walk with the swagger of a white man."

"I can walk like a Lakota. As for my feet, no one will see I am barefoot if we stay in the dark shadows."

"You do not smell like a Lakota. You smell white. If my people do not notice, the dogs will."

"Let us find out." Fargo took her arm and started down. He hunched at the waist enough to reduce his height by several inches, and held the blanket so it hung over his head and both sides of his face. "Walk close to me. Pretend we are lovers."

"You are very brave. But you are not very smart."

As they drew near the first circle, it dawned on Fargo that he had never seen the Sioux acting so out-and-out happy. He had witnessed victory celebrations and attended dances, but this was different. There was an air about them, as if they were caught up in great joy. The only thing he could compare it to was when whites attended a carnival and indulged in feasting and merrymaking.

As if she could read his thoughts, Sweet Flower said, "Look at my people. Their hearts are filled with gratitude for the great gift Wakan Tanka has given them. The white buffalo is a sign of the Great Spirit's favor. We will be strong, and defeat our enemies."

Fargo had never been a big believer in signs and wonders but he didn't argue the point.

Sticking to the shadows, they came by a circuitous route to the circle that included Little Face's lodge.

Hugging the deeper dark between tepees, Fargo averted his face whenever a Lakota came near them. For her part, Sweet Flower strode along calm and casual. No one would suspect she was sneaking a white man into their village.

"What will you do when we get there?"

Fargo hadn't thought that far ahead. He spied three horses with saddles outside the lodge. One belonged to Owen, the second was the sorrel Lichen rode, the third mount must be the senator's. At least Keever hadn't brought Rebecca and Gerty along.

"Be careful," Sweet Flower suddenly whispered.

Several Lakotas were coming toward them. Warriors, talking and smiling. When they were near, one of them raised a hand in greeting. "*Was'te.*"

Fargo knew it was Lakota for" greetings." He was about to respond but Sweet Flower beat him to it.

"*Hou.*"

The same warrior looked at Fargo, apparently expecting a reply, so Fargo said, "*Toniktuki hwo,*" which was "How are you?"

"*Nahan rei wayon heon,*" the warrior said, and laughed.

That was Sioux for "I am still alive." Fargo grunted and turned his head and walked on by.

Sweet Flower glanced over her should. "You can breathe easy. They did not catch on that you are not one of us."

"Take me around to the back of your father's lodge."

"If we are seen some might wonder why we are there."

"Not if you stand under the blanket with me." Fargo averted his face again as an old man came around a lodge and shuffled past.

They reached her father's tepee. Fargo raised the blanket and she did as he wanted, whispering, "They will banish me if they catch us."

"Not if I say I forced you." Fargo leaned toward the lodge and strained to hear. Muffled voices gave him no clue to what they were talking about. He recognized Little Face's voice, and then Owen's. "You should go in and hear what they are saying."

"My father told me not to come back until the whites leave. He will be mad if I go against his wishes."

Fargo reckoned he should take some consolation in the fact the senator was still alive.

"Careful!" Sweet Flower whispered.

Fargo heard footsteps behind them.

Sweet Flower suddenly threw her arms around his neck and kissed him, hard. He responded, savoring the feel of her body. The footsteps faded and she stepped back.

"I have become as bold as you."

"I like bold." Fargo peered out to be sure the person had gone, then bent and put an ear to the lodge. He still couldn't hear what was being said although he did catch a few words. Little Face talked, and then Owen, who was translating for Senator Keever.

Sweet Flower tapped him on the arm and he straightened. A group of warriors were going past. Again she kissed him, and from under the edge of the blanket he saw one of the warriors nudge another, and laugh.

"If we keep this up you will have to make love to me before you go," she teased.

"Thank you for what you are doing."

"I do it for my people." Sweet Flower touched his chin and wistfully smiled. "And for me."

Voices rose from the front of the lodge. Fargo realized those inside were coming out. He wanted to move closer but if Little Face spotted him, all it would take was a shout to bring every warrior in the village down on his head. Saddles creaked, and words were exchanged, followed by the thud of hooves as the white men rode off.

Sweet Flower rose onto her toes to whisper, "Follow me but stay out of sight." She moved around the lodge.

Fargo trailed after her and heard her address her father.

"May I go in now?"

"Yes. I am sorry if I offended you when I asked you to leave."

"Did it go as you wanted, Father?"

Little Face laughed. "Better than I dared hope. Whites are stupid, daughter. Deceiving them is easy."

"I am surprised you let them live."

"You must learn patience. There is no enjoyment in killing an enemy quickly. I learned that as a boy. I would pluck the legs off grasshoppers and hold them in my hand while they wriggled and tried to jump. I would catch butterflies and pluck their wings. I would shoot animals in the leg with my arrows just to watch them roll in pain."

"You never told me this."

"There was no need. But if I had killed this Kee-ver tonight, I would deprive myself of greater enjoyment tomorrow. I have invited him to a feast. The fool has promised to bring his woman and their child. Owen will come, and that other one, Li-chen. I will invite some of my friends, and after we eat and drink, we will fall on the whites and kill the men. The woman will be mine."

"What about the little girl?"

"She is too young to interest me. If no one else wants her, I will feed her to the coyotes."

Sweet Flower was quiet a bit. "Father?"

"Yes, daughter?"

"I am not sure this is wise. I worry what the rest of the whites will do. Blue coats will come. Many of them."

"Let them. A white buffalo has been born. That is a sign, Lame Deer. A sign that we will unite and drive the whites from our land for all time."

"I hope you are right."

"You doubt me?" Little Face sighed. "I should expect as much. You have always thought your own thoughts, even when those wiser than you think differently."

Fargo put his hand on his Colt. He could end it, now. All it would take was one shot. He started around the lodge but stopped at the sight of warriors approaching. In the lead was an older warrior who greeted Little Face warmly, and they all went into the tepee.

Sweet Flower hurried around. "You heard?"

"I will explain to Keever and lead him and the others out

of the Black Hills. Your father's plotting will have been for nothing."

"Then I will never see you again?" Sweet Flower asked, not hiding her disappointment.

"We are bound to cross paths." Fargo kissed her on the cheek and said softly, "You are a fine woman. I am proud to call you my friend. If you ever need my help you have only to ask."

"I will walk you from the village."

"That is not necessary." Fargo pulled the blanket around his shoulders. "Until we meet again."

"Until we meet again, He Who Walks Many Trails."

Fargo moved around the circle, staying in the shadow as before. None of the many Lakotas moving about noticed him, or if they did, thought anything of it. He was almost to the opposite side when a four-legged shape came out of a patch of ink and barred his path. He went to go past it.

The dog sniffed and growled.

"Good boy," Fargo said quietly in the Lakota tongue. He made no sudden moves that might provoke it.

The dog sniffed louder, and growled louder. A big yellow mongrel, it had short, bristly hair, and a lot of muscle.

Just what Fargo needed. He held himself still, waiting for the dog to make up its mind.

Hooves drummed. Mounted warriors were crossing the circle. They were not coming Fargo's way but they would pass within thirty feet of where he stood.

The dog took a step and bared its fangs.

Fargo started to hike his leg to get at the Arkansas toothpick. A silent kill was best.

The dog barked. A single bark would not attract much attention. But if the dog kept it up, the Lakotas would wonder why.

Fargo froze, hoping that if he stood completely still, the dog would stop.

It didn't. Crouching, it barked in a frenzy.

Out in the circle, Lakotas were looking. The mounted warriors heard, too, and reined around.

"Damn." Fargo was so close. He swung wide to go around and heard a Lakota shout. Something about "who are you and why is that dog making so much noise?"

Fargo didn't answer. He took another step.

And the dog sprang.

17

Fargo shot it. He cleared leather and fanned the hammer
when the dog was in midair. The blast kicked the Colt in his
hand and the slug slammed the dog back. It fell on its side,
howling stridently, and flopped about. Fargo had no lead to
spare to finish it off, and no time if he wanted to. He ran.

Yipping and yelling, Lakotas converged on the rear of the
tepee. The mounted warriors were first to get there. They
saw the dog, and slowed. Then, at a bellow from one of their
number, they jabbed their heels and galloped into the night,
spreading out.

By then Fargo had raced a good forty yards. Stopping, he
crouched low and pulled the blanket all the way over him. In
the dark he might be mistaken for a boulder, or so he hoped.
Warriors went by on either side, but none close.

Fargo stayed still. He heard more hooves, a slow clomp
that seemed to be coming right toward him. Pivoting, he cast
the blanket partly off. It was well he did. A warrior with a
lance was almost on top of him, the lance cocked to throw.

Fargo fired twice, coring the man's chest. The warrior
started to pitch over the side of his mount, and Fargo helped
him by grabbing an arm and yanking. Before the horse could
collect its wits, Fargo was astride it and reining toward the
rise.

Shouts from several quarters warned him other warriors
were coming.

Fargo bent low. The blanket went flying from his shoulders, flapping like an oversized bat. He let it go. He could always get another. His hide was harder to replace.

A warrior hove out of the gloom. Apparently he mistook Fargo for a Lakota because he called out, asking if Fargo had seen an enemy. Fargo answered "No!" and kept on riding. He was relieved when the rise appeared. At the top he vaulted down to reclaim his boots. He spent precious seconds pulling them on, then flew to the Ovaro.

In the saddle, Fargo raced from the vicinity of the village. He thought he had gotten clean away, and smiled.

Then hooves hammered, and there was a banshee screech.

Fargo looked over his shoulder. Three warriors had spotted him and given chase. He lashed the reins and the Ovaro went all out.

An arrow flashed over Fargo's head. It didn't miss by much. One of those warriors was an exceptional archer.

Fargo didn't shoot. He had no hankering to kill more Lakotas. They were only protecting their village from an intruder. On he rode, the Ovaro gradually widening its lead until at last the warriors were so far behind, they gave up the chase.

Fargo drew rein. The night was silent save for the heavy breathing of the stallion and the distant cry of a wolf.

"We did it, big fella."

Fargo patted the Ovaro's neck, noted the position of the North Star, and reined to the southeast. He had a lot of time to think on the long ride back to camp. He wondered about Keever not telling him the real reason the senator wanted to come to the Black Hills. That business about it being a secret––did the government really distrust him that much? Fargo couldn't see it being the case. He was friends with a fair number of high-ranking officers, including a general or two.

Fargo speculated that maybe it was something personal. But what it could be eluded him. It was puzzling. Even more so since the senator knew he spoke the Lakota tongue even better than Owen, and could help with the interpreting. The thought occurred to him that maybe Keever wanted to keep him out of it for that very reason, but that was ridiculous.

At last Fargo reached the valley. Two campfires were crackling, small fires, thank God. The senator, his wife and daughter, and Owen and Lichen were seated around one. Clymer and Harris and the rest of the men were at the other. All of them rose when Fargo rode into the circle of firelight and wearily dismounted.

Rebecca was the first to reach him. "Where have you been? We've been so worried."

"I was a guest of the Sioux."

Senator Keever was holding Gerty's hand but he let go and shouldered through the others. "What's that you just said? You've been where?" He glanced at Owen, who made an odd sort of motion with his hand.

"We have talking to do, Senator. But first I need something to drink." Fargo slid his tin cup from his saddlebags, went over to the fire, and filled it with steaming black coffee. He sipped gratefully as they gathered around.

"What happened to your face?" Rebecca asked. "You look as if you suffered a terrible beating."

Gerty squealed in delight and clapped her hands. "Oh, I hope he did! It would serve him right for being so mean to me."

"Hush," Rebecca snapped. "That was rude."

"Did you hear her, Father?" Gerty squealed. "Did you hear the tone she used with me?"

"I'm your mother," Rebecca said. "I can use whatever tone I like."

"You're not my *real* mother. My *real* mother wouldn't treat me the way you do. My *real* mother would be nice."

Fargo shocked them by growling, "Shut the hell up, you little brat."

Owen slapped his leg and cackled. "That's telling her! Better yet, take her over your knee and whale the living daylights out of the hellion."

"Enough!" Senator Keever declared. "I won't have you or anyone else show such blatant disrespect for my family."

"We have something more important to talk about," Fargo enlightened him. "Whether you want to leave now or wait until first light?"

"I beg your pardon?"

Fargo took another sip. "You're being played for a jackass, Senator. Little Face isn't interested in a peace treaty. I've just come from his village. I was outside his lodge when you were inside talking to him."

Keever gave a start as if he had been pricked with a pin. "You were? What did you hear?"

"Not much. But that doesn't matter. What does is that he has no interest in peace. He wants to count coup on a chief of the whites. Guess who that is?"

"Preposterous. This meeting was his idea. He got word to Mr. Owen and Mr. Owen got word to me. Little Face wouldn't go to all this bother just to kill me."

"A Sioux warrior lives to count coup. The more coup he counts, the more brave deeds he does, the more he is looked up to, and respected. If Little Face counts coup on you, a great white chief, he will stand high in Lakota councils."

The senator waved his hand as if dismissing the very idea. "If he wanted to kill me he could easily have done it tonight when I paid him a visit."

"Get it through your head. He's the cat and you're the mouse." Fargo forgot how stubborn Keever could be. "And he asked you to bring your wife and daughter with you tomorrow, didn't he?"

"What?" Rebecca said.

Keever bobbed his chin. "As a show of good faith. For his

part, he's invited leaders of all the bands. It's most fortuitous they have gathered to celebrate the white buffalo."

"What is this about taking Gerty and me?" Rebecca demanded. "You never said anything to me."

"Come now, my dear. It's no different than a dinner engagement back in Washington. Only we will be dining with uncouth red savages and not the elite of society."

Fargo said, "You're not dining with anyone."

"I'm afraid that's not your decision to make. You are in my employ, not the other way around. And there's another factor to be considered."

"What the hell are you talking about?"

Senator Keever smiled. "You needn't concern yourself about it. I have matters well in hand."

Fargo was fast losing his temper. There was just no reasoning with some people. "Like hell you do. I can't let you go. I can't let your own stupidity get your wife and the brat killed, too."

Gerty snapped, "Take that back."

"Thank you," Rebecca said.

Keever looked bored. "How considerate. But when I say I have matters in hand, I truly do. That pathetic heathen only thinks he's outwitted me, when the truth is, I've outwitted him."

"I'll ask you one more time," Fargo said harshly. "What the hell are you talking about?"

Owen cleared his throat. "You know, Senator, maybe now is the time. I know we haven't heard yet, but why run the risk of him spoiling things after you've gone to so much bother?"

"An excellent point," Senator Keever said. "Very well. Do what must be done."

To Fargo, none of this was making any sense. It made even less sense when Owen drew his six-shooter and pointed it at him. A second later Lichen did the same. "What the hell?"

Keever chuckled. "I'm afraid you must undo your gun belt and hand it over or these gentlemen have my permission to—what is the quaint expression? Ah, yes. They have my permission to fill you with lead."

Rebecca put a hand to her throat. "Fulton! What on earth has gotten into you?"

"All in good time, my dear," Keever said airily. He jabbed a finger at Fargo. "Well? What will it be? Hand over your Colt, or die. The decision is yours."

Lichen took deliberate aim. "I hope he gives us an excuse. I've wanted to buck this son of a bitch out for weeks now. Always acting better than us and bossing us around."

Owen didn't say anything. He just stood there and smirked.

Fargo undid his belt buckle. It wasn't as if he had a choice with them covering him.

The other men looked on in amazement. Clymer found his voice first and asked, "What's going on, Senator? We didn't sign on for anything like this."

"Everything will be explained to you shortly," Keever assured him. "For now it is enough that you know I was sent by the government to work out a peace treaty with the Sioux and this man intends to stop me."

Clymer scratched his head. "Why would Fargo do a thing like that?"

"Ask him yourself after we've cut his claws." Keever held out his hand. "The Colt, sir, and don't try my patience."

Boiling with anger, Fargo handed his gun belt over.

"Thank you." Keever stepped back. "Now, Mr. Owen, if you please, would you and Mr. Lichen escort Mr. Fargo to my tent and see to it that he can't interfere with my plans?"

Lichen slipped around behind Fargo and jabbed him in

the back. "You heard the man. Keep your hands where I can see them or I'll blow a hole clean through you."

The confusion on the faces of Clymer and Harris and some of the others was mirrored by Fargo's own. For the life of him, he couldn't figure out what Senator Keever was up to.

Owen parted the tent flap and Lichen prodded Fargo and told him to get down on his knees with his hands behind his back. Then Lichen put the muzzle to his head.

"Be back in a minute," Owen said, and went out.

Lichen snickered. "You lived with the Sioux once, I hear tell."

"For a while," Fargo admitted, thinking the weasel might reveal what this was all about.

"They must have put a lot of trust in you. But they won't after the senator is done. No sir. They'll want to stake you out and skin you. Or maybe make you run one of those gauntlets I've heard about, where they stand in two rows with knives and tomahawks and you have to run between them."

"They only do that to their worst enemies."

"Which is exactly what you'll be." Lichen gouged the muzzle hard into Fargo's skin. "They'll hate you more than they've ever hated anyone. And they won't be the only ones. Likely as not, the Cheyenne and the Arapahos and other tribes will want to carve on you, too."

"Why?"

The flap opened and in came Owen carrying a rope. He set to work tying Fargo's wrists.

"Well, look at this. Someone beat me to it. You've been rubbed raw." Owen deliberately scraped the rope against Fargo's open flesh hard enough to draw blood, then looped it tight and tied a knot. "If that hurts, let me know and I'll tie it tighter."

His jaw muscles twitching, Fargo endured the pain. His ankles were bound, and he was shoved onto his side.

Lichen hiked a boot to stomp him in the face.

"No," Owen said.

"Why not? He's as good as dead anyway, once the Sioux find him."

"You heard me."

The flap parted again. Wearing an oily smile, Senator Keever came over. "How pathetic. You have no idea what I'm about, do you? Not the faintest suspicion?"

"I figure you're after gold," Fargo admitted.

"Oh, please. As rich as I am? I wouldn't waste my time." Keever moved to a cot and sat. "Permit me to enlighten you."

"Just don't talk me to death."

"Very well. First off, I'm not here on behalf of the United States government. They didn't send me to arrange a peace treaty. My business in the Black Hills is strictly personal."

"What business?"

Keever adopted a condescending tone. "Can't you guess yet? What's the one thing I love to do more than anything else in all the world?" He chuckled. "I'll give you a hint. Remember the trophy room I'm so proud of?"

An explosion went off in Fargo's head. In a burst of insight he divined the truth. "God, no. You can't mean—?"

"But I can, and I do. I'm here for one reason and one reason only. To kill the white buffalo."

18

Skye Fargo had seen and done a lot in his time. It was rare that anything shocked him. But this did. He gaped in stunned bewilderment at Senator Fulton Keever and then blurted his uppermost thought. "You're loco."

"Not at all."

"Do you have any idea how much blood will be shed if the Sioux find out a white man shot it?"

"Do you have any idea how little I care?" Keever smiled. "I'm a hunter, Mr. Fargo. Not of typical game, either. I hunt the biggest, the rarest, the most dangerous. They are the only trophies worth having. And I think you'll have to agree with me that hanging the head of a white buffalo on my wall will be the crowning achievement of a lifetime."

Fargo's initial shock had passed and he thought of something. "You don't know where it is so how can you shoot it?"

"Mr. Owen has offered a young warrior a shiny new rifle and all the ammunition the warrior can carry for that very information. He's due here any time now. Once he tells us, Mr. Owen and Mr. Lichen and I will slip away. It will be the greatest hunt of my life."

"As for the Sioux blaming a white man," Owen said, "we want them to. We even have a particular white man in mind."

Keever leaned back and laughed. "That look on your face is priceless, Mr. Fargo. You must have a million questions. So ask away. I have time to spare until the buck gets here."

The hell of it was, Fargo *did* have a lot of questions. He started with the obvious. "When did this harebrained idea come to you?"

"When Mr. Owen contacted me to tell me of Little Face's peace proposal. He happened to mention how excited the savages were over the birth of a white buffalo. It got me to thinking. No one, anywhere, has a white buffalo head on their wall. I'd be the first. It would make me the talk of Washington."

"So you sent word to Little Face that you'd meet with him but you only came to shoot the buff?"

"An accurate assessment. I've used him. But remember, Little Face has been using me, as well. He never intended to sign a peace treaty. By your own admission he brought me here to kill me." Keever chuckled. "Turn about is fair play, yes? By tomorrow night I'll have my trophy and be on my way out of the Black Hills."

"You took a gamble going to see him tonight."

"Not really. I don't trust any of these red heathens any further than I can throw that bear we killed. I had a derringer up my sleeve, and Mr. Owen and Mr. Lichen were armed."

"Kill the white buff and the Sioux will be outraged. They'll comb these hills from end to end. They'll find you and your trophy before you can hope to get away and do things to you that would curl your hair."

"That they would, yes," Keever agreed, "if they thought I was to blame. But you see, that's the beauty of my plan. I have a scapegoat. Actually, an excess of scapegoats. There's you, and Rebecca, and all the men in camp."

"What?"

"Oh, yes. You see, the warrior who is coming to tell us where to find the white buffalo will go back to his village and say that he saw you and a bunch of other whites chasing it. I would imagine the Sioux will be terribly incensed. So much so, they will undoubtedly swoop down on this camp and wipe out everyone in it without giving any of you a chance to speak in your defense."

"You miserable bastard."

"Please. Spare me the flattery. But I do have it planned out to the smallest detail, if I say so myself."

"Why did you pick me out of all the scouts?"

Keever winked at Owen. "That was his doing. I confided in Mr. Owen from the very beginning. When I suggested we needed someone to divert the Sioux from us, he mentioned you. It seems he and you have never gotten along all that well, and this is his way of paying you back."

Owen nodded. "The other reason I suggested you is because you've lived with the Lakotas. They trust you. If you brought the senator in, they'd figure he was really here to talk peace."

Without any warning, Lichen rapped Fargo's head hard with the revolver. "How does it feel to be so stupid? You're going to die and there's not a damn thing you can do about it."

Fargo grimaced with the pain. He had to stall. But the only thing he could think of to say was, "Why kill Rebecca? What did she ever do?"

Keever placed his elbows on his knees and his chin in his hands. "To be frank, I weary of her. Our marriage has always ever been one of convenience, and the convenience has worn thin." He let out a sigh. "She's never really loved me, you know. She did it for the money. Not that I minded. I married her so my constituents would think I'm an upstanding pillar of the community. But the truth is, I like to have a different woman every other night." He leaned toward Fargo. "Just as she likes a different man. You're but the latest in a long string. Did she feed you that line about not having sex? She uses it a lot."

Footsteps approached the flap. Lichen jammed his revolver against Fargo and put a finger to his lips.

Outside the flap, Harris said, "Senator Keever, sir? Is Owen in there? There's a Sioux here to see him. He doesn't speak good English but he says Owen is expecting him."

Owen answered, "Tell him I'll be right there."

"What perfect timing!" Keever exclaimed, and rose. "Mr. Lichen, gag our friend, if you please."

"What do you want me to gag him with?"

Senator Keever took a handkerchief from a jacket pocket. "How about this? I only used it once to blow my nose."

Fargo's stomach did a flip-flop. "Try it and I'll bite your fingers off."

In a twinkling, Owen had a knife out and pressed the edge to Fargo's throat. "Be a good little scout and sit real still. There's no reason you have to be alive when the Sioux show up."

"Don't you think they'll wonder about me being tied?"

"They'll be so mad, they won't much care. My guess is they'll start in on you the minute they find you." Owen smiled. "I'd love to be here to hear you scream."

Lichen gripped Fargo's chin. Fargo resisted, but only until Owen pressed harder with the knife. The handkerchief tasted of sweat, and worse.

"There!" Lichen said when he had tied Fargo's own bandanna over Fargo's mouth to keep the gag in. He stepped back. "That should do."

"A lamb for the slaughter," Senator Keever crowed. "Let's hurry, gentlemen. We shouldn't keep our visitor waiting any longer than we have to."

The three men filed out.

Fargo told himself it could be worse. They had been careless, and that carelessness would cost them. Twisting, he looked down at his boot. By bending as far back as he could, he was able to hike his pant leg and slide his fingers into his boot to palm the Arkansas toothpick.

A slight sound caused Fargo to look up. A shadow was

silhouetted against the flap. Quickly letting go of the knife, he moved his bound hands away from his boot.

In crept Rebecca. "I knew it!" she said in horror. She bent and pried at the knots. "I saw them walk off. We might not have long."

Fargo grunted and wagged his head, trying to get her to remove the gag, but she went on prying.

"Be still. I'll get you free. I don't know what this is about but my husband has no right to do this." Rebecca moved to a corner of the tent where several packs were piled. "There's a hunting knife around here somewhere."

Fargo rubbed his mouth against the ground in an effort to loosen the bandanna. He was still rubbing when the flap opened again and in walked Senator Keever, holding a derringer.

"Well, well. What are you up to, my dear?"

Rebecca froze, her hand in one of the packs. "Fulton! I thought I saw you go off toward the horses with Mr. Owen."

"You did. But unfortunately for you, I looked back and saw you sneaking in here."

"Don't be absurd. Why would I sneak into my own tent?"

"Because you were worried about your latest lover." Keever wagged the derringer at Fargo.

"I'm sure I have no idea what you are blathering about." Rebecca got off her knees, and turned.

Keever trained the derringer on her. "That will be far enough, my dear. I'm afraid I've reached the limits of my patience with you and your betrayals."

"Me?" Rebecca flushed red and balled her fists. "What about you? What about all the nights I've slept alone while you've been off with other women?"

"I have a weakness. I admit it. But I've paid you well, haven't I? And it's not as if I didn't explain the conditions of our relationship when I asked you to be my wife."

"Wife!" Rebecca scornfully barked. "In name alone. The only reason you took me as yours was to hide your indiscretions, and like a fool I've kept quiet all these years."

"Recriminations, my dear, get us nowhere."

"Stop calling me that." Rebecca took another step but stopped when the derringer's hammer clicked. "You wouldn't dare."

"On the contrary. I've had Mr. Owen spread talk among the men about how unhappy you are with me. I didn't have him say why but he gave the impression you were tired of being married and would do just about anything to be on your own. Anything at all."

"No one would believe that."

"Why not? These men don't know you. Who is to say you didn't come at me with a knife and I was forced to shoot you in self-defense?"

Rebecca appeared genuinely stunned. "Are there no depths you won't plumb?"

"Wait until you hear the rest. But first, have a seat." Keever motioned at the cot, and when she obeyed, he looked at Fargo and then at her, and chuckled. "Two birds with one stone. This is quite marvelous."

"What do you intend doing with him?" Rebecca demanded.

"The same thing I intend doing with you. In his case, the Sioux will do it for me. In yours, I'm afraid Mr. Owen and Mr. Lichen will take you out and dispose of you."

"You're having them *kill* me?"

"I'll blame it on the Sioux, of course. The newspapers will eat it up. A senator's wife slain by savages. I'll be the perfect portrait of a stricken spouse. The sympathy alone should gain me a lot of votes in the next election."

Fargo was beginning to realize that the senator was one of the most dangerous men he ever went up against. He supposed he shouldn't be surprised. Politicians didn't have the best of reputations. He just never imagined they could be such vicious bastards.

The flap opened again. Fargo twisted, expecting Owen and Lichen, but it was the pint-sized rattlesnake.

"Gerty!" Rebecca exclaimed. "Quickly. Go fetch Mr. Harris and the other men. Tell them I need to see them right away."

Gerty smiled sweetly at the senator. "Should I, Father? Should I do as my *pretend* mother wants?"

They both laughed, and the daughter went over and put her arm around her father.

"My God," Rebecca breathed.

"Must you always be so melodramatic?" Keever criticized her. "All of us die. It's just a question of when."

Rebecca didn't give up. She appealed to the girl, saying, "Did you hear him, Gerty? Your father plans to murder me, and to have Mr. Fargo killed by the Sioux. You must tell the men. Not Owen or Lichen but the others. Run, child. Our lives are in your hands."

"Isn't she funny, Father?"

"Gerty?" Rebecca said.

"All the times I've told you and you didn't hear me." Gerty put her hands on her hips and glared. "I *hate* you. I wish you were dead. Father says that soon you will be, and I'll have a new mother when we get back." She giggled in delight. "I can't wait."

All the blood drained from Rebecca's face. "How could I have been so stupid?"

"Oh, please," Keever said in disgust. "You brought this on yourself. All you had to do was play the good wife. But no." He patted Gerty on the shoulder. "Would you be a dear and go see what is keeping Mr. Owen?"

"Certainly, Father."

But the girl had hardly taken a step when in came the man in question and his shadow.

"Well?" Senator Keever prompted.

"Bear Claw was as good as his word. The white buffalo is with a herd about half a day's ride west of here."

"You're sure you can find it?"

"Easy as pie. Lichen and I will take the first watch. As soon as the others are asleep, we can slip away. You'll have your trophy by tomorrow night. I guarantee."

Keever beamed. "I couldn't be more pleased. You have done excellent work, and you'll be properly rewarded."

"All of you are unspeakably vile," Rebecca said.

The senator sighed. "Mr. Lichen, would you be so good as to bind my darling wife? No need to be gentle with her. In fact, I insist you tie her so tight, it cuts off her circulation."

"My pleasure."

Rebecca bolted, or tried to. She shoved Lichen and was almost past the senator when Gerty flung out a foot and tripped her, spilling her hard onto her hands and knees. Owen's revolver arced, and at the *thud* of metal on her head, Rebecca collapsed.

Fargo swore through his gag.

Smiling, Keever placed his hand on Gerty's head. "You did fine just then, my dear."

"Anything for you, Father." Gerty looked at Rebecca and then at Fargo. "Anything that gets these two dead."

19

Skye Fargo was a keg of black powder set to explode. He had been tricked, used, and beaten. He had been lied to and led around like a bull with a ring through its nose. Worst of all, he was being set up to take the blame for a heinous act that would see the prairie run red with blood.

Lichen bound and gagged Rebecca and dragged her to the back of the tent. Drawing a knife, he cut a long slit, hooked his hands under her arms, and hauled her out, wriggling to squeeze through the canvas.

Senator Keever was acting extremely pleased with himself. "I'd leave my darling wife here with you, you understand, but I can't run the risk of the Sioux not killing her. Some buck might take it into his fool head to take her for his woman, and the next thing, word would get out and the army or someone else would barter to get her back. So we dispose of her now."

"How?" Fargo asked through his gag.

"What's that? Did you ask how? I've left that up to Mr. Lichen. Just so he does it quick and gets back before I leave to go shoot the white buffalo." Keever smoothed his jacket. "Come along, Gerty. We'll go sit by the fire. We must do as we normally would until all the rest are asleep."

"Yes, Father."

Owen went to follow them and paused at the flap. "You won't believe this, hoss, but I'm sorry it has to be like this. You and me, we're a rare breed. We're one of a kind."

If not for the gag, Fargo would have said that there was a big difference between them. He had a few scruples; Owen didn't have any.

"And in case you're wondering, I'm doing this for the money. The senator is paying me ten thousand dollars. I lead him to the buff, I get him out of the Black Hills safe and healthy, and I have more money than I've ever seen at one time in all my born days."

All Fargo could do was glare.

"For what it's worth, I argued with him over having the Sioux kill you. I'd as soon do it myself. Quick and clean. Not because I like you but because no white man deserves to die as you're going to die."

The flap closed, and Fargo was alone. He wasted no time. With a heave of his shoulders he was up on his knees. He slid his fingers under his pant leg and down his boot. A tug, and the Arkansas toothpick was out of its sheath. Carefully reversing his grip, he cut at the rope binding his wrist. The rope was thick but the toothpick was razor sharp. The instant the rope parted, he sliced the loops around his legs.

Quickly, Fargo dashed to the back of the tent and squeezed through the slit. The woods were quiet save for the sounds from their camp. Staying low, he worked around toward the horse string. All the horses were there. Which meant Lichen had dragged Rebecca off on foot. They couldn't be that far.

Fargo turned into the woods. It could be Lichen was going to kill her close to camp so that later, if anyone came to investigate and found her remains near the site of the massacre, they'd assume the Sioux had killed her, too.

Yes, the more Fargo thought about it, it sounded like something Senator Keever would do. The man was as crafty a bastard as ever drew breath.

Every sense alert, Fargo wound through the trees. He was afraid that in the dark he would miss them. He went fifty feet, a hundred, a hundred and fifty. A rustling noise to his left gave him hope. He slowed. On cat's feet he stalked around a blue spruce. For a few seconds he couldn't make sense of what he was seeing. There appeared to be someone lying on the ground. But it wasn't one person, it was two.

Rebecca was on her back. She was still bound and gagged.

Stretched out next to her, freely running his hand over her body, was Lichen.

"Stop it, damn you. Try to knee me one more time and so help me God, I'll slit your damn throat and be done with it."

Rebecca tried to shout through her gag but all she managed were throaty gurgles.

"And stop that, too. They can't hear. It's just you and me. Your husband gave me permission to do whatever I please, and it pleases me to have some pleasure before I feed you to the worms."

Fargo edged forward. He was in the open but Lichen's back was to him.

"I've got to hand it to that husband of yours. He doesn't miss a trick. It must come from all the conniving and finagling he does for a living." Lichen placed a hand on her breast. "Mmm. Nice and full, like cantaloupes. I like that. I like cantaloupes better than apples any day." He chortled at his joke.

Fargo had only a yard to go. Lichen had taken his Colt but he didn't see it anywhere.

"If you're smart you'll let me have my way. The more I'm enjoying myself, the longer I'll let you live."

The pale starlight glistened off tears on Rebecca's cheeks.

"Oh, hell. Don't start that. If there's anything I hate worse than a bawling female, I've yet to come across it."

Rebecca uttered a soft sob.

"Damn you. It's not as if I'm about to do something you haven't done with a hundred other men, if what the senator says is true. He told us you feed them a lie about not having made love for five or ten years so they'll take pity on you. Is that how it goes?"

Fargo was close enough. He slowly bent, his arm that held the toothpick as rigid as iron.

Lichen drew his knife. "I'm going to cut your legs free so you can spread them wide. But act up, do anything, anything at all, and I'll kill you where you lie." He bent and slashed the rope cleanly with one stroke, then pressed the tip of his blade against her ribs. "I'd like to undo that gag so we can swap kisses but all it would take is a shout from you and those other lunkheads would come on the run." He kissed her ear, her neck, and squeezed her breast. "You are one mighty fine woman, if I say so myself. It's too bad your husband won't let me keep you for my own." Lichen pushed her dress up above her knees, placed a hand on her leg, and taunted. "Do you know what happens next?"

"You die," Fargo said.

Lichen glanced up in surprise.

Quick as thought, Fargo struck. He buried the toothpick to the hilt in Lichen's left eye socket. At the same time, Fargo rammed a knee into Lichen's mouth and then his throat to stifle any outcry.

Lichen lurched up off the ground. He was only halfway to his feet when he let out a long, slow breath, and deflated. He twitched, gurgled, and died.

Fargo tried to pull the toothpick out but it wouldn't budge. Bracing his boot on Lichen's chest, he wrenched with both hands. Not only did the blade come out, the eyeball came with it.

Rebecca rolled onto her side and made noises while thrusting her wrists at him.

"Hold your horses." Fargo shook the toothpick to dislodge the eyeball but it clung fast. He tried again, harder, and this time the eyeball went flying—onto Rebecca's cheek. She squawked like a strangled chicken and tossed her head to shake the eyeball off. Instead, it oozed toward her mouth.

"Stay still."

Rebecca looked fit to faint.

Fargo plucked it from her and tossed it into the dark. Lichen's shirt was as good a place as any to wipe his fingers. Then he cut her loose.

Pushing to her feet, Rebecca was female wrath incarnate. "That son of a bitch husband of mine! Where is he?"

"Not so loud. We don't want him to hear us."

"I don't care if he does or he doesn't. He's dead. Do you hear me? Dead, dead, *dead*!"

Fargo clamped a hand over her mouth but the harm had already been done. He heard footsteps fading rapidly and spied a dim figure racing toward camp. He had a good idea who it was: Owen, come to see what was taking Lichen so long. "Come on." He started to give chase but he took only a few steps when Rebecca called his name.

"Don't leave me! Please."

Reluctantly, Fargo stopped. She was limping and held a hand out for him to help her. "What's wrong?"

"I came to when that worm was dragging me from the tent. I tried to fight him and he kicked me in the knee. I can barely walk."

Fargo slipped an arm around her and she leaned against him. "We have to hurry. Hop with your good leg." He moved as fast as she could bear to go without falling on her face. But it wasn't anywhere near fast enough. He was sure the senator and Owen would be gone by the time he reached the camp, and sure enough, three horses were missing from the string.

All the men were sound asleep, their snores loud enough to wake a hibernating bear.

Fargo let go of her. "As soon as I leave, wake them up. Tell Harris he's in charge. He's to pack everything and get the hell out of here. Head south. I'll catch up later."

"Wait." Rebecca clutched his arm. "You're going after them alone?"

"I can make better time." And, Fargo reflected, one rider was less likely to be spotted by the Sioux.

"What will you do when you catch them?"

"What do you think?" Again Fargo tried to leave but she held on to him.

"Fulton is a United States senator. He has many powerful friends in Washington. Do you have any idea what they'll do to you if they find out?" Rebecca answered her own question. "They'll crucify you."

"Only *if* they find out."

"Oh." Rebecca nodded, then rose onto the toes of her good foot and kissed him on the cheek. "For luck."

His spurs jangling, Fargo sprinted to the Ovaro. Vaulting onto the saddle, he reined to the west. Half a day's ride, Owen had said. Or half a night. The problem was that "west" included a lot of countryside.

Fargo rode hard for the first fifteen minutes. He kept hoping he would catch a glimpse of Owen and Keever, or hear them. But he didn't, so he slowed to spare the Ovaro. It wouldn't do to exhaust the stallion so soon. He had a feeling he would need to rely on its speed and stamina before too long.

It was then that Fargo thought he heard another horse. Drawing rein, he listened, but the sound wasn't repeated. His imagination, he reckoned, and gigged the Ovaro on.

At night the Black Hills truly were. Mounds of ink, framed by a myriad of stars. From all points rose the howls and shrieks and roars and wails of the wild things, the cries of the meat-eaters and the plant-eaters the meat-eaters preyed on.

Fargo decided to climb a hill. From the summit he might spot them. He was halfway up when, once again, he thought he heard horses—behind him. Drawing rein, he waited for the sounds to be repeated but when a minute went by and they weren't, he clucked to the Ovaro.

In broad daylight it would have been easy to spot riders at a distance. But at night all Fargo saw was an unending vista of black and more black. He swore and started down the other side. Then, as clear as could be, he heard the *chink* of a hoof on stone. This time there was no mistake. It wasn't his imagination.

He was being followed.

Fargo drew rein and slid down. He left the Henry in the saddle scabbard. At close range in the dark the Colt was just as effective. Drawing it, he crept to the top of the hill.

Riders were climbing toward him.

Fargo counted five but it was hard to be sure. One of them whispered—in the Lakota tongue.

"Go slow and stay quiet. He cannot be far ahead."

The whisperer was Little Face.

Fargo smiled a cold smile. He crouched, and waited, and when they were almost to the top he centered the Colt on a darkling figure. The revolver spurted flame and lead and the figure let out a sharp cry. Quickly, Fargo shot two more, blasting them from their mounts in the time it took to blink.

That left Little Face and one other, both of whom gave voice to war whoops, and charged.

Fargo slammed off a shot from the hip. The other warrior threw up his hands and tumbled to the dirt.

Little Face kept coming, his arm cocked to hurl a lance.

Diving to the right, Fargo rolled. He'd only had five pills in the wheel, which meant he had only one left. He must make it count.

The lance thudded into the earth next to him.

Fargo looked up. Little Face loomed large against the night sky, seeking to trample him under the driving hooves of his mount. Fargo pointed the Colt, and shot. He swore he heard the smack of the lead that knocked Little Face headfirst to the ground.

The horse didn't stop.

Fargo quickly reloaded. None of the warriors were moving except Little Face, who was on his side, thrashing and gurgling. Fargo walked over. With his boot he flipped Little Face onto his back. The shot had caught him in the chest and a fine mist was spraying from the bullet hole. "Can you talk?"

"Finish me."

Fargo bent over him. "How did you get on my trail?"

Little Face sucked in a deep breath. "There was a commotion in our village. A white man was seen. I went to where I had left you with Long Forelock and Bear Loves and found them dead."

"And?" Fargo prompted when he didn't go on.,

Little Face sucked in another breath. "I knew you would try to warn the sen-a-tor that I wanted to count coup on him. So I gathered some friends who hate whites as much as I do, and we came to your camp. Just as we rode up, we saw you leave."

"And you came after me to kill me." Fargo straightened. He aimed at the center of Little Face's forehead and thumbed back the hammer. "Any last words?"

"I hate you."

The boom of the Colt rolled off across the hills. Fargo replaced the spent cartridge, twirled the revolver into his holster, and strode to the Ovaro. "Three to go," he said.

20

The Black Hills covered a lot of territory. Thousands of square miles, Fargo had heard. Even narrowing down the area where the white buffalo might be to the western half left a lot of ground to cover.

Fortunately, the Black Hills were not all hills. There was rolling grassland where buffalo grazed and wallowed, and Fargo was willing to bet every dollar in his poke that that was where he would find the white buff.

The problem, though, was that the grassy tracts were widely scattered. He couldn't check all of them in one night. Or seven nights. His best bet was to cover as much ground as he could and hope for a stroke of luck.

Fargo was a big believer in Fair Lady Chance. She often favored him at cards, and she certainly liked to toss ladies in his lap. A friend of his once said that he was born under a lucky star. Fargo wouldn't go that far, but he would admit that nine times out of ten, luck worked in his favor. As any gambler would confirm, those were uncommonly high odds.

Still, Fargo couldn't stop worrying. If he didn't find Keever in time, open warfare would break out. The Lakotas and other tribes would be incensed. To them a white buff was a symbol of all that was good. When they found out a white man was to blame for the calf's death, they would join forces and rise up in a wave of slaughter the likes of which the West had never seen. Hundreds would die.

Unless Fargo stopped Keever.

So Fargo rode. He rode hard. He pushed the Ovaro as if their lives depended on it. He was alert for sounds or the telltale glow of a campfire. But on the one night he most needed Lady Chance to smile on him, she was over at a corner table playing roulette with someone else.

The notion brought a weary chuckle to Fargo's lips. He still had his sense of humor.

The minutes added up into hours and the hours crawled toward dawn. A pink blush decorated the eastern horizon when Fargo drew rein on a flattop hill and gazed in all directions. Disappointment left a bitter taste in his mouth. He had tried and he had failed. Soon it would be daylight, and Senator Fulton Keever would add another trophy to his wall.

Fargo swore. He considered going to his friend Four Horns and asking his help. The only thing was, he had no idea where to find Four Horns' village.

It seemed like everything was against him.

Then a thin golden crown framed the rim of the world, and the gloom of night was relieved by the gray of dawn. Fargo arched his stiff back, and yawned. He was all set to ride on when, far in the distance, he saw four-legged sticks. His pulse quickening, he rose in the stirrups. There were three of them. They were too far off to tell much but it had to be Keever and the brat and Owen.

Fargo fought down a burst of elation. They were miles away. Overtaking them before they shot the buff was asking for a miracle.

"Sorry, big fella," Fargo said as he pricked the Ovaro with his spurs. "I know you're tuckered out."

The golden crown became a ring and the ring became a yellow plate. All around, the shadows of night were dispelled by the spreading light of the new day.

Fargo came out of the woods to the belt of grass where he had seen the riders. He slowed and twisted in the saddle, desperate for some sign. But there was nothing, nothing at all.

A rifle boomed and a leaden bee buzzed his ear. Another inch over, and the grass would have been spattered with his brains.

Fargo reined around and streaked toward the woods. He wasn't worried so much for his own hide as for the Ovaro's; the smart thing for the shooter to do was to bring the stallion down.

Again the rifle banged but the rifleman rushed his shot and the slug clipped the stallion's flying mane.

Fargo glanced over his shoulder. A puff of gun smoke let him know the rifleman was hidden in the high grass. Drawing his Colt, he fired three times. He didn't expect to draw blood. He wanted the man to hug dirt long enough for the Ovaro to reach safety.

It worked.

Swinging down, Fargo shucked the Henry. He darted from trunk to trunk until he was at the last one. Cautiously, he peered around, and nearly lost the top of his head to a shot that left a deep furrow in the tree and peppered him with slivers of bark.

"Almost got you that time, didn't I?" Owen shouted, and cackled.

Fargo took his hat off and set it on the ground. "Where did the senator get to?" He had a notion Keever left Owen there to keep him busy while Keever went after the white buffalo.

"He's up ahead a ways," Owen replied. "To get to him you have to get past me."

"Is he paying you extra for this?" Fargo kept him talking while peeking out again.

"As a matter of fact, he is. Two hundred to keep you from interfering. Five hundred if I blow out your wick."

"A lot of gents have tried."

Owen laughed again. "Haven't you heard? There's a first time for everything."

Fargo saw grass move sixty yards out. Owen was changing position. He took a bead low to the ground, and fired. A startled oath greeted the shot.

"Damn you! That pretty near got me in the hip."

"I'll try harder next time." Fargo worked the lever, feeding another cartridge into the chamber. The Henry held fifteen in the tubular magazine under the barrel. As folks liked to say, you could load a Henry on Sunday and shoot it all week.

The grass was moving again.

"You could make this easy on both of us," Owen hollered. "You could get on that fine animal of yours and light a shuck. No one will ever know."

"Except me." Fargo wedged the stock to his shoulder. All he needed was a gap in the grass.

"Damn it. Be reasonable. What's the white buff to you?"

"To the Indians it means a lot."

"Why are you so bothered about a bunch of savages? And so what if they get upset? It's just a buffalo, for God's sake. Another white one will come along in ten or twenty years and they can make a fuss over it."

"Lichen is dead, you know."

The grass stopped moving. "I figured as much. You told me that to make me mad, didn't you? Hoping I'd jump up like an idiot and start spraying lead. But I'm not that stupid."

"Stupid enough." Fargo had discerned a vague shape that might or might not be Owen. He thumbed back the hammer, took precise aim, and lightly stroked the trigger.

At the *crack* there was a roar of pain. Owen's rifle spanged, four, five, six times. He was a good shot. The trunk was struck again and again.

Fargo chuckled. He worked the Henry's lever and leaned

his shoulder against the tree. "Almost got you that time, didn't I?" he mimicked Owen's earlier taunt.

"You *did* get me, you son of a bitch! Nicked my leg. It hurts like hell."

"Show yourself and I'll try to do better." Fargo scanned the nearest trees and spied a spruce that suited his need.

"Funny man. But this isn't doing you any good. You might as well leave while you still can. By now Keever has the herd in sight. It shouldn't take him long to pick out the white buff. Any minute now we'll hear the shot."

Flattening, Fargo crawled toward the spruce. Now if only Owen didn't spot him.

"What's the matter? Cat got your tongue? You've gone to all this trouble, and for what?"

Fargo crawled faster. He went around the tree and rose into a crouch. The lowest limb was within easy reach. He pulled himself up, branch after branch, until he had climbed twenty feet.

"Answer me, damn you."

Fargo parted two limbs. And there was Owen, on his belly in the grass. Snail-slow, Fargo slid the Henry's barrel between the limbs and rested it on the lowest. He lined up the rear sight with the front sight and both sights with Lem Owen.

"What are you up to in there? Are you trying to flank me?" Owen turned his head right and left.

Fargo waited for him to stop.

Owen cast a puzzled look at the trees, then cupped a hand to his mouth. "Are you still there?"

Fargo fired. He jacked the lever and went to take aim again but Owen was prone, both arms flung out. Quickly, Fargo descended. He couldn't see Owen. If he'd only wounded him, Owen might be waiting for him to show himself. But he couldn't afford more delay. He sprinted out into the grass.

Lem Owen was still there, still facedown. There was no need to roll him over to confirm he was dead. Much of the top of his head was gone, and his brains were oozing out.

Fargo ran to the Ovaro. He mounted and rode past the body. Fifty yards on was a hollow and in it was Owen's horse. Now all Fargo had to do was backtrack to where Owen had parted company with Keever.

The grass was dotted with droppings. There were scores of wallows. A lot of buffalo had been this way.

Fargo worried that he had miles to go and would be too late. Then he remembered. Owen said something about being able to hear the shot. Keever couldn't be that far.

A low rise rose like a serrated saw. Fargo goaded the Ovaro up it but stopped short of the rim. Sliding down, he crept to the crest. He smelled them and heard them before he saw them: hundreds of shaggy brutes, most grazing. A few bulls pawed the ground. Calves gamboled playfully about.

Nowhere was there sign of a white one.

Fargo turned to the right and the left. The rise went for hundred of yards in both directions. He saw no one and was about to stand and walk to the Ovaro when a head popped up two hundred yards away. A head with white hair.

Stooping so low his nose practically brushed the ground, Fargo glided toward it.

It was Keever, all right, and his attention was fixed on the herd.

Fargo glanced in the same direction, and tensed. There it was—the white buffalo. If Fargo had to judge, he would say it wasn't much over six months old. It was said that buffalo nursed until seven or eight months, and that was what this one was doing. It made a perfect target.

Fargo threw caution to the breeze, and ran. Keever would hear him but he didn't give a damn.

Oblivious to its danger, the white buffalo continued to nurse.

The senator had his eye to the tube above the barrel. Any moment now and he would shoot.

Fargo took a few more bounds and stopped in his tracks. *What the hell was he doing?* he asked himself. There was an easy way to foil the bastard. Grinning at his inspiration, he pointed the Henry at the sky and banged off eight shots while whooping like a Comanche on the warpath.

Shaggy heads rose in alarm. Bulls bellowed and cows snorted, and the next thing, the entire herd was in motion. Every last buff wheeled to the south and joined the stampede, the white buffalo and its mother among them.

"Nooooo!"

Senator Keever was on his feet, staring after the fleeing buffs in consternation. He jerked his rifle up but he didn't have a shot. So he ran after them, yelling at the top of his lungs. A crazy stunt, since he had no hope of catching them. He was almost to the bottom of the rise when a giant brown shape rose up out of a wallow.

"Keever!" Fargo shouted, but the senator couldn't hear him over the din. Fargo snapped the Henry up but before he could shoot the bull was on its intended victim.

At the last second Keever must have heard it. He spun, directly into the bull's path. A curved horn caught him full in the chest and he was swept off his feet as if he were weightless. A toss of that great head, and the senator went flying. He tumbled shoulders over heels and flopped to a stop. The bull didn't slow. It ran to join its fellows, one horn black, the other horn glistening red.

Fargo went to see. There was nothing he could do. The hole was big enough to shove his fist through. Keever's eyes were wide in terror and would stay that way this side of eternity.

The drum of hooves brought Fargo around in a crouch. This time it wasn't a buffalo; it was Gerty, quirting her horse, her young face twisted in fury. She rode right at him, screaming, "I'll kill you! Kill you! Kill you! Kill you!"

Fargo dodged, grabbed a leg as she swept by, and up-ended her. He felt no sympathy when she bounced a few times. She was unhurt and swearing like a river rat as he forked her under his arm and carried her to the Ovaro.

"Let go of me, you wretch! Where are you taking me?"

"You'll find out soon enough."

It took three nights of searching. The woman with the withered face was half a mile from the village, flitting among the trees. She gave a start when Fargo rode up and dumped the bundle at her feet.

"You!" she exclaimed. "I remember you."

"I bring you a gift."

She stared at the blanket. It was tied at both ends and bulged and moved as if alive. "What is this?"

"The girl you have been searching for."

The woman titled her head. "She does not sound like Morning Dew."

"Keep her anyway." Fargo touched his hat brim and used his spurs. He didn't look back.

LOOKING FORWARD!
The following is the opening
section of the next novel in the exciting
Trailsman **series from Signet:**

THE TRAILSMAN #334
COLORADO CLASH

Colorado, 1861—three men dead, a town filled
with ugly secrets and Fargo trying to stay alive long enough
to learn the truth.

Skye Fargo might not have found the body if he hadn't decided to stop by the creek and fill his canteen.

Late September in Colorado was a melancholy time with the thinness of the afternoon sunlight and the snow-peaked mountains looking cold and aloof.

Ground-tying his big Ovaro stallion, Fargo grabbed his canteen from his saddle and walked through buffalo grass until he came to the narrow, winding creek. The water was clean. He hunched down next to it, opening his canteen. A jay cried. Fargo looked over to see what the hell was wrong with the damn bird.

And that was when he saw, sticking out from behind a ponderosa pine to his right, a pair of boots. Easy to assume that attached to those boots was a body.

He finished filling his canteen before getting up and walking through the smoky air to stand over the remains of what appeared to be a teenager of maybe sixteen, seventeen years. From the denim shirt and Levi's and chaps, Fargo figured that the kid had been a drover. Cattle were getting to be a big business around here.

The birds had already been at him pretty good. The cheeks reminded Fargo of a leper he'd once seen. One of the eyes had been pecked in half. Dried blood spread over the front of the kid's shirt. Hard to tell how long the kid had been here. Fargo figured a long day at least. The three bullets had done their job.

He found papers in the kid's back pocket identifying him as Clete Byrnes, an employee of the Bar DD and a member of the Cawthorne, Colorado, Lutheran church. Cawthorne was a good-sized town a mile north of here. That was where Fargo had been headed.

He stood up, his knees cracking, and rolled himself a smoke. He'd seen his share of death over the years, and by now he was able to see it without letting it shake him. The West was a dangerous place, and if bullets weren't killing people, then diseases were. But the young ones got to him sometimes. All their lives ahead of them, cut down so soon.

The cigarette tasted good, the aroma killing some of the stench of the kid's body.

Not far away was a soddie. He walked toward it and called out. Then he went to the door, but there was no answer.

He went back to his Ovaro then, untying his blanket and carrying it back to the corpse. He spread the blanket out on the grass and then started the process of rolling the body on it. Something sparkled in the grass. He leaned over and picked it up. A small silver button with a heart stamped on it. Something from a woman's coat. He dropped it into his pocket.

When the blanket was wrapped tight, he hefted the body up on his shoulder and carried it over to the stallion. He slung it across the animal's back and then grabbed the rope. A few minutes later the kid was cinched tight and Fargo was swinging up in the saddle.

Two minutes later he was on his way to Cawthorne.

Karen Byrnes had no more than opened the door and stepped inside when she saw the frown on Sheriff Tom Cain's face. She knew she was a nuisance and she really didn't give a damn.

A regional newspaper had once called Sheriff Cain "the handsomest lawman in the region." Much as she disliked the man, she had to give him his bearing and looks. Sitting now behind his desk in his usual black suit, white shirt, and black string tie, the gray-haired man had the noble appearance of a Roman senator. It was said that he'd always looked this age, fifty or so, even when he was only thirty. It was also said that many gunfighters had mistaken the man's premature gray for a slowing of his abilities. He'd killed well over two dozen men in his time.

The office was orderly: a desk, gun racks on the east wall, wanted posters on the right. The windows were clean, the brass spittoon gleamed and the wood stacked next to the potbellied stove fit precisely into the wooden box. Tom Cain was famous for keeping things neat. People kidded him about it all the time.

The hard blue eyes assessed Karen now. She tried to dismiss their effect on her. Somehow even a glance from Cain made her feel like a stupid child who was wasting his time.

"There's no news, Karen."

"Been two days, Tom."

"I realize it's been two days, Karen."

"They found the other two right away."

"Pure luck. That's how things work out sometimes."

She had planned to let her anger go this time. She would confront him with the fact that if her brother Clete was dead that would make three young men who had been murdered in Cawthorne within the past month. And the legendary town tamer Tom Cain hadn't been able to do a damn thing about it. The father of one of the victims had stood up at a town council meeting and accused Cain of not being up to the task of finding the killer. He had immediately been dragged out of the meeting. In Cawthorne nobody insulted Tom Cain. When he'd come here four years ago, nobody had been safe. Two warring gangs of outlaws held the town for ransom. Many of the citizens had started to pack up their things and leave. To the shock and pleasure of everybody, Cain had needed only five months to set the gangs to running. Eleven of them were buried in the local cemetery. It was downright sacrilegious to insult Tom Cain.

"My mother's dying, Tom. You know that. Her heart's bad enough—if we don't find Clete—"

He stood up, straightened his suit coat and came around the desk. Just as he reached her, she began to cry—something she'd promised herself she wouldn't do. He gathered her up and took her to him, her pretty face reaching well below his neck. He let her cry and she resented it and appreciated it at the same time.

"We're all just so scared, Tom. Especially my mother."

His massive hand cupped the back of the small blond head and pressed it to him.

"I'm going to find him, Karen. I promise you that. And I'm going to find out who killed the other ones, too. I haven't had any luck yet but I think that's going to change."

She leaned away from him, looked up into the handsome face. "Did you find out something?"

"I don't want to say anything just yet, Karen. I don't want to have bad luck by talking about it."

Despite the situation, she smiled. That was another thing they always said about Tom Cain. Him and his damn superstitions.

"Excuse me," said the slim older deputy Pete Rule, coming through the door that separated the four cells in back from the front office. Rule wore a faded work shirt. A star was pinned to one of the pockets. There was a melancholy about Rule that Karen had always wondered about. Cain's other deputies were basically gunslingers. She wondered why somebody as quiet and often gentle as Rule would have signed on. "Afternoon, Karen."

"Hello, Pete," she said, slipping from Cain's arms. She'd liked Rule ever since she'd seen him jump into a rushing river and pluck out a two-year-old girl who'd wandered into it.

"We'll find him, Karen," Rule said. "That's a promise."

Karen nodded, a bit embarrassed now that she'd been so angry.

"You tell your mother she's in my prayers," Cain said.

"Thanks for helping us. If you weren't here—" She felt tears dampen her eyes again.

"You better go get yourself one of those pieces of apple pie that Mrs. Gunderson's serving over to the café for dinner tonight," Cain said. "She snuck me a slice, and I'll tell you, I felt better about things right away. And I suspect she'd let you take a piece home for your mother, too."

At the door, she said, "If you hear anything—"

"We'll be at your door ten seconds after we get any kind of word at all."

She nodded to each of them and then left.

"I know one thing," Rule said. "He ain't alive. He's just like them other two."

"Yeah," Cain said, almost bitterly. "And when we find him, I'll be the one who has to tell her."

A little girl in a dress made of feed sacks was the first resident of Cawthorne to see the body of Clete Byrnes. She had just finished shooing her little brother inside for supper when she turned at the sound of a horse and there, passing right by her tiny front yard, was a big man on a stallion just now entering the town limits. She knew that there was a man in the blanket tied across the horse because she could see his boots. She wondered if this was Clete Byrnes. Her dad knew Byrnes from the days when he'd worked out at the Bar DD. Byrnes was all her dad talked about at the supper table the past two nights. He said he figured Byrnes was dead but then her mother got mad and shushed him for saying that in front of the four children.

She waved at the big man on the horse and he waved back. Then she ran inside to share her news.

Cawthorne had once been nothing more than a cattle town, but these days it was a commercial hub for ranchers and farmers from all around. Fargo started seeing small, inexpensive houses right after he waved to the little girl. He traveled the main road from there into town. At indigo dusk, the stars already fierce, the mountain chill winterlike, he reached the three-block center of Cawthorne. Most of the false-fronted businesses had closed for the day but two cafés and four saloons were noisy as hell and obviously planned to stay that way.

Every few yards somebody on the plank walk would stop to peer at him. There was a fair share of buggy, wagon, and horse traffic but somehow, even before they saw the blanket on the back of the Ovaro, they seemed to know that this was the horse everybody in town had been dreading to see.

They had to wait until Fargo came closer to confirm what they suspected. Then they jerked a bit at the sight of the blanket or cursed under their breath or said a prayer.

Fargo watched for a sign identifying the sheriff's office. He had to pass by the saloons before reaching it. A couple of whores stood on the porches of their respective saloons. Fargo had known enough of them in his time—and had liked a hell of a lot of them—to know that these two had stepped out just to get away from the cloying stench and grubbing hands of life inside.

The sheriff's office was at the end of a block that fronted on a riverbank. The building was long, narrow, adobe. As he dismounted and started to tie the reins of his Ovaro to the hitching post, he turned to see shadow shapes in the gathering darkness. The word was out. Only a few of those in the business district knew about Clete Byrnes as yet but soon most of Cawthorne would. A half dozen shadow shapes hurried down the street toward Fargo. The first wave of ghouls.

He walked up to the door and shoved it open. A gaunt man in a faded work shirt and a star came around the desk. "Everything all right?"

Fargo noted that the man's first instinct wasn't to go for his gun. A good sign. Too many gun-happy lawmen around.

"I've got a body out here. His papers said his name is Clete Byrnes."

"Oh, damn, that poor family of his. What happened to him?"

"He was shot three times."

Fargo walked back out on the plank walk. By now twenty people had formed a semicircle around the Ovaro and its lifeless passenger. Men, women, even a pair of tow-headed kids who might have been twins. An elderly gentleman with a cane carried a smoky lantern that he held up to the corpse.

8678

"Did somebody say it's Clete? I always knew that boy'd end up like this."

"Well, that's a hell of a thing to say," a woman wrapped in a black shawl snapped. "And I'll remember it when we bury you, too. I'll have some choice things to say then, my-self."

A few of the people laughed, making the scene even stranger.

The deputy shouted, "Now you get away from here and get on about your business."

"We got a right to be here, Pete. Same as you do."

"Is that right, Sam? I guess I can't see your badge because it's so dark. But maybe somebody made you a deputy with-out me knowing it. We need to sort this thing out."

"Who's the one who brought him in?"

The deputy offered Fargo his hand. "Pete Rule."

"Skye Fargo," the Trailsman said as they shook.

"Hey, I've heard of him!" one of the men said.

"Now, c'mon, folks. This whole situation is bad enough. Just please go on about your business."

They left resentfully, calling Rule names as they shuffled away.

Cold moonlight gave Rule enough of a look at the face of the corpse to know who he was seeing. "It's Clete, all right." He shook his head. "Third one in a month."

"Any idea if they're connected?"

"That's what the sheriff is trying to figure out. They were friends, hell-raisers, but they never got into any serious trou-ble. That's what makes this whole thing so damned strange. Who'd want to kill them?"

From down the street came the clatter of a buckboard. All Fargo could see of the man driving it was a top hat. Who the hell would wear a top hat in a town like Cawthorne?